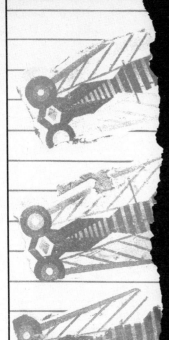

Jack Gantos

HEADS OR TAILS

Stories from the Sixth Grade

A Sunburst Book
Farrar Straus Giroux

LIBRARY OF CONGRESS CATALOGING-IN-PUBLICATION DATA
Gantos, Jack.
    Heads or tails : stories from the sixth grade / Jack Gantos. —
1st ed.
        p.   cm.
    Summary: Jack's diary helps him deal with his problems which
include dog-eating alligators, a terror for an older sister, a
younger brother who keep breaking parts of himself, and next-door
neighbors who are really weird.
    ISBN 0-374-42923-5 (pbk.)
    [1. Diaries—Fiction.   2. Family life—Fiction.   3. Schools—
Fiction.   4. Humorous stories.]   I.   Title.
PZ7.G15334He   1994
[Fic]—dc20   93-43117

To my mother and father

CONTENTS

COPYCAT

CREPT UP ON my diary. Carefully, I undid the lock with the small key I kept on a string around my neck, then slowly opened it.

"Ughhhh," I moaned. The pages were filled with squished spiders. I slammed it shut like a tiny coffin.

It wasn't the spiders that scared me. I had pressed them into the book. It was all those blank pages. For *three years* I had been trying to fill them, but I could never think of anything interesting to write. It was as though my brain stopped working if I even thought of my diary.

This didn't make sense. Usually, I was pretty good at imagining things. When I looked at the picture of the sailboat on my wall, in my mind I could see Dad racing the Flying Dutchman yacht of his dreams. When I read a good book, like *The Feathered Serpent,* the words filled my brain with people, smells, and sounds. But when I opened my diary, my mind went as blank as the paper. I felt like a moron.

It started the afternoon Mom came home from work and gave my older sister, Betsy, a diary. The year was stamped in gold on the flowery front cover. The hundreds of pages were made of thick, glossy paper. But what amazed me most was the lock. A strap from the back cover fit into a lock sewn onto the front cover, and there was a tiny key that only Betsy would be able to use.

"You can write anything that comes to your mind in this book," Mom told her. "A diary is for keeping all your secrets, and nobody is allowed to read it but you."

I looked up at my mother. "Where's mine?" I asked.

"I'll get you one when you're old enough to have secrets," she said.

"I do have secrets," I shot back.

"Not *grownup* secrets," she replied.

"I *want* a diary," I shouted and stomped my foot as hard as I could.

Mom didn't budge so I had to go all the way. I threw myself down on the floor and cried and bucked up and down. "I *want* a diary! I *want* a diary!"

"Don't be such an immature little brat," Betsy said and walked off to her bedroom, probably to start filling her diary with secrets. I howled even louder and kicked the floor with my heels.

"Okay, cut the theatrics," Mom said. "I'll get you a diary, but you must promise to write in it every day."

I promised. But I did not keep my promise.

At first, I just wrote down what day it was and the weather. Then I started listing everything I ate. But when it came to writing about what I was doing or what I was thinking and feeling, I couldn't seem to get it down. I could lie in bed and remember everything I had seen and said during the day, but when I opened the diary my thoughts vanished.

Still, I fought back and began to fill my diary with *stuff*. Each day, I searched for interesting things. I captured all kinds of bugs and squished them between the pages. I stapled in my baseball cards. I kept my stamp collection neatly arranged in rows. I used the diary as a photo album and mounted all my pictures inside. When I taped in my fortune-cookie fortunes, they looked like tiny telegrams from a foreign land. One of them read, "You Are Brave And Have Many Friends." I didn't believe it. I was covering over the empty white space of the pages in the same way I covered my eyes with my hands when I watched a monster movie.

It was no good. Even though the diary was filled with stuff, it was stuff someone else had thought up, someone else's *stuff*.

This evening was no different. Without writing much of anything, I locked the diary, grabbed a deck of cards and fled my bedroom. Betsy was sitting at the dining-room table playing a hand of solitaire. I sat down across from her and began to lay out my cards.

"Stop that," she said sharply.

"What?" I said.

"Stop copying me," she said. "Mom, tell him to stop copying me. He's driving me crazy."

"Leave your sister alone," Mom said, "and come help me work on this jigsaw puzzle. I'm having trouble."

Betsy slapped her cards down on the table. "Don't let him help you, Mom," she said. "Make him think of something to do on his own. Everything I do, he wants to do. Everything you do, he wants to do. He doesn't have a brain in his head. He's like some kind of dumb animal. Monkey see, monkey do."

"That's enough," Mom said. But we knew Betsy was right. I couldn't come up with any great ideas of my own. Nothing seemed interesting until I saw another person do it first. When Betsy started a shell collection, I started a shell collection. When she put PEACE posters on her bedroom wall, so did I. I wanted to be friends with all her friends. It seemed as if I could only do what she did first. I'll never be the President, I thought, just the Vice President. I won't be a gangster kingpin, just his stooge. I won't be the sole survivor in any humongous disaster, just another victim along with all the other losers. Believe it or not, I hate feeling sorry for myself. It makes me feel like an idiot, which makes me feel even sorrier for myself.

"Why don't you go fishing with your father," Mom suggested.

Dad was in the back yard, fishing in the canal for mullet and reading his favorite magazine, *Popular Mechanics*. But a few days before, I had seen our left-side next-door neighbor, Mr. Velucci, feeding spoiled pork chops to the alligators in the canal and I didn't want to go near that brown water. And I didn't want to get into a dumb discussion with Dad on how to transform his truck into a cabin cruiser or the washing machine into a helicopter. *Popular Mechanics* gave him the strangest ideas.

"Dad and I have nothing in common," I said, repeating a line I had heard Betsy say the previous week.

"Don't you have any homework to do?" Mom asked.

I did. I was avoiding my math homework because I wasn't

sure of the assignment. My teacher terrorized me and I was afraid to ask her after school for an explanation. I didn't know the other kids that well and I was afraid to ask them. They might call me *stupid*. And once you get that name you're stuck with it for the rest of the year.

My teacher's name was Mrs. Marshall and I thought she was more dense than I was. *She* certainly didn't have an original thought in her head. Each day, after she took roll, she turned to us and announced, "All students take out your copybooks." We reached under the seats of our desks for our black-and-white composition books. But we didn't dare open them until she said so. She had threatened to mash our fingers between the pages if we disobeyed.

From a desk drawer she removed a pair of white cotton gloves and put them on. Next she got a fresh box of white chalk from her supply closet and loaded five new sticks into her wire chalk holder which drew five lines at a time. She pressed it against the chalkboard in front of the class and scratched a stack of lines from left to right. The screeching was so loud I thought my head would explode. Then she scratched more lines across the blackboards that ran along the entire right side of the room and across the back. Along the left side of the class, we had windows. But Mrs. Marshall wheeled two portable blackboards in front of the windows and our room became gloomy. She covered them with lines, too. I was surrounded by walls of blackboards, and from where I sat the gray lines of chalk looked like miles of barbed wire.

She removed a textbook from her desk and opened it to the page where we had left off the day before. She held the book in her left hand and raised a piece of chalk with her right. "Students, prepare to copy," she ordered. We opened our copybooks and twenty-five ballpoint pens clicked into position. "Go," she shouted and began to write. She copied onto the board exactly what was written in the book. If I only had known what the title of the book was, or who wrote it, I would have bought it so I could copy it at home. But she kept the book wrapped in a brown-paper cover.

"Egyptian history begins with the reign of King Menes," I scribbled.

She wrote like a sewing machine. Her handwriting looked even better than my mother's. All the letters were perfectly formed and they all slanted to the right at exactly the same angle. My handwriting was a mess. I wrote mostly straight up and down. My letters were always squashed together or too large and loopy. But, worst of all, I was slow. Every day I tried to keep up with Mrs. Marshall, but when she finished filling up the front blackboard I was only halfway down. She made us keep our desks clustered together in the center of the room so she had space to use the boards. When she finished the front, she hollered, "Shift!" and we scooted our desks a quarter turn to the right and faced the long side blackboard. Because I hadn't finished the front, I left a section of my copybook blank and began with the new board. I figured that maybe I could get caught up later. "Shift!" she hollered when she finished the side board and moved to the back, and again we scooted our desks to the right. When I looked around, it seemed that all the other kids were keeping up with her. Then she began on the portable blackboards.

"Shift!" she commanded. We did, and once again I left extra space in my copybook as I leaped ahead of myself, trying to keep up. But I was still scribbling away when she finished the portable blackboards. She put down her book and chalk and quickly began to erase her writing as I desperately scrambled to fill the blank spots in my book. When all the boards were erased, she said, "Everyone put down your pens and stretch out your fingers and hands." As the class stretched, a team of honor students jumped into action. They wet sponges in the back sink, then madly washed the chalkboards. The room was so hot the water evaporated in a flash, and once again we were ready to go.

"Okay," she announced after drawing fresh lines. "Everyone pick up your pens and let's begin." She changed books and we began to copy a chapter on earth science.

All day long we copied chapters from her books, but I never remembered a thing I wrote. I was too frazzled with trying to keep up. At the end of the day she had overlapped me a dozen times. I felt even more tortured each Friday, when we turned in our copybooks. She passed them out to us on Monday and each time I read the same comments: "Write more neatly and quickly. Don't daydream. Keep your mind on your work." What mind, I asked myself. I didn't have a thought of my own.

Betsy scooped up her playing cards. "You can play cards," she said. "I'll do some homework." She got up and went to her bedroom.

I picked my cards up, too, and ran to my bedroom. I grabbed my book bag and dashed back to the dining-room table before Betsy had returned. I took out a clean sheet of paper and a book.

When Betsy returned she slapped her books down on the

table. "Copycat," she sneered. She spread her homework out while I copied a page from my history book. After a while I peeked up at her to see what she was doing. She was writing a letter to a friend. It occurred to me that I should be writing a letter to a friend. Then I noticed that she was writing differently than usual. Her handwriting slanted to the left instead of to the right. I thought it was a neat idea and so I started to do it, too. I was peeking up at her again to see if I was missing out on some new trick when she saw me.

"You're copying my new handwriting," she said. "I caught you."

"I am not," I cried. She snapped up my paper before I could grab her hand. "Give it back," I hollered. "I'll call Mom."

"Call her," Betsy said calmly, "so I can show her what a moron you are. Not only are you copying my handwriting but you are copying your homework word for word out of the book. A trained monkey could do what you do."

"Leave me alone," I said.

"Gladly." She sighed and gathered up her books. "If you try to follow me into my room, I'll knock you cold and sell you to a zoo."

I didn't care what she said. I was excited with the new handwriting style. It seemed to work really well for me. My letters were clear and I thought I was writing faster. I couldn't wait to try it out in class.

The next morning I got up early and started to get dressed. Everyone at school was wearing blue jeans and T-shirts. But Mom had other ideas. At the beginning of the school year she took me to Sears and bought five new pairs of slacks, five matching shirts, five pairs of matching socks, and a pair of brown lace-up shoes. Then she organized my closet so that on Monday I wore the green slacks and green-and-yellow plaid shirt with green socks. On Tuesday, I wore the brown slacks with the brown-and-white stripes and brown socks. This was Friday, so I put on my blue slacks and the blue-and-white checkered shirt with dark blue socks. Getting dressed was like being on an assembly line. I couldn't wait until I was old enough to pick out my own clothes. Mom said it had nothing to do with being old enough. "When you can *pay* for them," she said, "you can wear whatever you want. You can go to class dressed in a clown suit."

Today I'm going to have an idea of my own, I promised myself as I rode my bike to school. I'm not going to copy Betsy. I'm going to do exactly what I want to do, no matter what anyone thinks of me. I can either be a copycat for the rest of my life or I can be a one-of-a-kind.

I passed the drive-in theater at the end of our street. They showed only old movies and *The Sound of Music* was still playing. It was playing when we moved into the neighborhood, and that was four months ago. On some nights when the wind was blowing just right, I could hear the music through my bedroom window. Because of that movie, I caught myself singing, ". . . The hills are alive . . ." about a million times a day. I heard it in my brain when I was sitting in class. I heard it when I was playing kickball. I heard it when I was eating breakfast. I hated that movie. Maybe that's why I don't have an original thought in my head, I guessed. I'm being brainwashed by that movie all night long.

I got to school early. The place looked as strange as ever.

It was made out of eight separate rectangular wooden trailers. There was one trailer for each grade, first through sixth. One trailer was for the office and one trailer was split in half for the girls' and boys' bathrooms. All the trailers were fitted with wheels and the entire school could be pulled away in the middle of the night. I could imagine all of us arriving one morning to find nothing but the asphalt paths left behind in the sandy field which was hot and large as a desert.

When Mrs. Marshall gave us the order to "start copying," I was ready for her. My new slant-to-the-left handwriting *was* faster. As she circled the room I was almost right behind her. And because I wasn't so afraid of being overlapped by her all the time, I could think about what I was writing. The Egyptians were great. Maybe I'll be an archaeologist when I grow up and study ancient Egypt, I thought. That was an original idea for me.

I went home for lunch and unlocked my diary with the key I kept around my neck. Yesterday I had scrawled above a line of flattened ants that I was "the stupidest kid on the planet." Today I wrote: "There is hope for me after all." The discovery of my new slant-left writing would change my life, like the discovery of electricity had changed the world, I decided. I closed the diary and heard the delicious crunching of a juicy palmetto bug that hadn't yet dried out.

At the end of the week, Mrs. Marshall collected our copybooks. I was excited because I had almost kept up with her the last two days, now that I was using my new handwriting. I expected praise for doing better. Maybe she'd even make me an honor student.

On Monday morning Mrs. Marshall handed out the

copybooks. I flipped through the pages, and when I reached my new writing, I saw a big red X across every page. "DO YOUR OWN WORK," she had written. "SEE ME AFTER CLASS." My heart was pounding. I tried not to cry, but I could feel the tears filling my eyes. I put my head down on my desk as Mrs. Marshall began to draw lines around the room.

At lunchtime I waited until everyone left the classroom before I went up to her desk.

"I don't respect cheaters," she said to me.

"But I did write this," I protested. "I changed my writing."

"Don't argue with me," she replied, "I've already made up my mind. I don't know who copied this into your book, but you can't fool me."

I didn't know what else to say. I was being cheated by my teacher and there was nothing I could do about it. I turned and walked to my desk.

"I expect from now on you'll do your own work," she scolded. "Let this be a lesson to you."

The rest of the afternoon I copied her as best I could in my old handwriting. She overlapped me five times. I imagined myself failing sixth grade because I was unable to write fast enough. Betsy was right. A trained monkey could do what I do, only better.

When I returned home I went straight to Betsy's bedroom. "You've got to help me," I blurted out. "Look at this." I opened the notebook and showed her Mrs. Marshall's comments.

"Well, that's what you get for being a copycat," she said.

"But I did do the work," I cried.

"What do you want me to do?" she asked.

"Write her a note and tell her I copied you," I begged. "She'll believe you."

"I'm not your mother," said Betsy. "You copied me, now suffer the consequences."

"But I promise never to copy you again. Cross my heart and hope to die."

"Even your promises are copies of promises," she said scornfully. "Beat it."

I retreated to my bedroom. I thought I could take a book and copy it in my new handwriting and prove to Mrs. Marshall that it was my work. But she could say someone else had done it, and fail me. I knew what I had to do. I unlocked my diary and with my new handwriting began to write down anything that came into my mind. I wrote between the bugs and stamps and cards and fortunes. At first, my writing didn't make sense. No two sentences had much in common. Then I suddenly began to write out all the lyrics to *The Sound of Music*. There were a lot of those songs stuck in my head. After I cleared them out, I settled down and started to write all about my lousy school year.

I woke up early and caught myself humming a few bars from *The Sound of Music* as I got dressed. It didn't seem to bother me as much.

I rode my bike up to the classroom door. Mrs. Marshall was in the back of the classroom washing out her white cotton gloves, and hanging them across a line she had strung over the sink.

"You're awfully early," she said, turning to look at me as she dried her hands on a towel.

"I wanted to talk privately with you," I said.

"I thought you might," she replied.

"This is my diary," I said and handed it to her. "I'm the only one with a key." I removed the string with the key on it from around my neck and held it out for her. "Go ahead and open it," I said. "You'll see my handwriting is the same."

She unlocked it. The pages fanned open and stopped at a gummy mouse skin I had peeled off the street. It still smelled fresh. "That's disgusting!" she cried and dropped the book. "Unsanitary!"

"But you can see my new handwriting," I said, retrieving the book. I held it open for her. "See, it slants left."

She glanced at it. "Yes," she snapped. "It's the same. Now go take your seat."

I sat down and flipped open the diary. It would be fifteen minutes or so before kids started filing in. I turned to a page with a squished beetle. I drew curly hair on it like Mrs. Marshall's. I added little white gloves on its arms and legs. I put a stick of chalk in each hand. I drew a blackboard covered with lines, and between the lines I wrote, in my new handwriting, "I won. I won. I won."

yelled really loud. I
kept thinking, OH
MY GOD hes going to
chop his finger off and
I'm going to have to
wrap it in ice and
get it to the
hospital!
Once I chopped
off a lizards tail.
It wiggled
like a ti
whi
it on
my
bere
it
Pete's fin
of my
wiggle to

MY BROTHER'S FINGER

IT WAS SATURDAY. I was standing outside our house looking down at a large brown patch on our dying front lawn. I was thinking of the two ladies I had overheard at the grocery store talking about the new "renters" who had just moved onto their street. One lady said that "renters" ruined the neighborhood because they never took good care of their lawns, never kept their houses properly painted, and always had ugly dogs. They weren't talking about us, but we were the new "renters" in my neighborhood. We had never owned our own home. Probably never would. Since I was born, we had already lived in nine different houses. I hated that word "renter." It made me feel that I didn't really belong anywhere, like we had to pay people to put up with us.

I needed some chinch-bug spray and was wondering how to get it. I looked at the house. It needed fresh paint all over.

The roof was moldy with Spanish moss and the split gutters were sagging. Everywhere I looked I saw something that needed to be fixed. The driveway asphalt was cracked and breaking up into large chunks. The grass along our section of the sidewalk had grown over the concrete. Beneath every palm tree was a scattered pile of dead palm fronds and coconuts, and all the flower beds needed reshaping and weeding. Maybe those ladies were right. We were a mess.

Dad came out of the house and waved to me. He had his binoculars around his neck.

"What are you doing today?" he asked. This was a trick question. If I didn't sound busy enough, he might think up new chores for me.

"I want to kill some bugs," I replied. "We have chinch bugs and if we don't spray them now they'll spread to the neighbor's lawn, then all of Fort Lauderdale, and then the whole state of Florida." I wanted him to fund the bug massacre. He lifted the binoculars to his eyes and focused on the brown patch of lawn as if he could see the minuscule bugs singing happy little songs as they chewed the roots off the grass. For five dollars I could change their tune.

"If we owned this property, I'd rip out the grass and lay down a slab of green concrete," he said, kicking at the dead spot.

Or gravel, I thought. He was always saying that it was so much easier to take care of concrete or gravel.

"But since we don't own it," he chirped, "we'll just have to keep it as best we can." I knew what was coming next as I watched his eyes scan the yard. "You'd better cut up the palm fronds and trim the shrubs around the property line and against the house. And if you mowed the lawn it would look better. Also, you can take the hand shears and trim along the sidewalk. That much we can do," he said, "we" meaning me. "And I'll give the landlord a call and tell him we have chinch bugs and have him spend his own damn money to get rid of 'em. After all, it is his yard."

"Okay," I said with a groan, knowing my chance for a big bug massacre was ruined. I started singing, "I've been working on the raillll-road, all my live-long days . . ."

He looked at his watch. "Got to go," he announced, as if he were on his way to an important business meeting. But it was chore day and he was sneaking away. I couldn't wait until I grew up so I didn't have to do anything I didn't want to do. I'd get married, have a bunch of kids, and make everyone work like dogs while I played golf or watched airplanes.

Before I was born, Dad owned a Piper Cub single-engine plane and used to perform his own stunts. He was known for his flying pranks. Once he landed on a baseball field during a game. Another time, he dropped water balloons on people coming out of church. After he buzzed my grandmother's house and sent her hiding in the basement, Mom made him sell the plane.

But he hadn't lost interest in flying, and each time we moved to a new town he always hung around the local airports and made friends with the pilots and mechanics.

"I better get going," he said. "Johnny's waiting for me to repaint the stars on his De Havilland biplane. The other guys are down there already, polishing up the body. Some Hollywood types are going to film him doing stunts for a movie."

He got into his pickup truck and drove off. I wished I could have gone with him. I'd love to get a ride in that biplane. But I was left behind to slave my butt off so Mom wouldn't complain so much about him ducking out.

I decided if I was going to have to work hard so was my little brother, Pete, but I knew I would have to bribe him first. He had just started first grade and the only chore he had was to keep his room tidy. Big deal! I was in sixth grade and old enough to do adult work for peanuts. My allowance was two dollars a week, and no tips.

Pete was in his bedroom playing with a plastic army jeep. It was his favorite toy. Each time he steered it over a little bridge, one of the tires pressed a hidden button that made the bridge explode.

"Don't you ever get tired of doing the same thing over and over?" I asked. "You're like a robot."

"Watch," he said and ran the jeep over the bridge. "Boom!" he shouted as the bridge tumbled and he threw the jeep into the air. It bounced off the ceiling and came straight down on his head.

"Ow," he whined. "That hurt."

"No kidding. Now let's get something to eat. Then we can play with my Zero." I yanked him up by his arm.

"Yay!" he shouted. He ran past me and danced down the hall toward the kitchen, forgetting all about his head.

For my birthday, Dad had given me a Japanese Zero that was powered by a small gasoline engine. I stunk at making it fly by myself. It took Pete and me to make it work. First I had to start the engine, then hand the plane to Pete, who held it by the fuselage while I dashed back to the string controls. "Now," I'd yell, and he'd run with the plane held over his head. When the guide strings were taut, I'd shout, "Let her fly!" He'd pitch it forward and the plane would climb as it curved around me. But I wasn't very good with the guide strings that worked the air flaps, and usually before the Zero made a complete circle, it nosedived into the sand. "Boom!" Pete would shout, and then he'd fall to his knees, laughing.

When I got to the kitchen Pete was standing on a chair. He had the peanut butter opened on the counter and the bread dealt out like cards. I got a banana from the fruit bowl and took jars of pickles and cocktail onions out of the refrigerator.

"Don't make a mess," Mom shouted from her bedroom. "I've already cleaned in there." She had ears like a rabbit.

"I'll make a deal with you," I said, slicing the pickles lengthwise. "If you help me with the yard work, I'll let you steer the plane."

"I want to start it," he said.

I didn't expect this. I had always started the engine by flipping the propeller with my finger. Each time I did it, I imagined I might not get my finger out of the way in time and it would get sliced up like a piece of pickle. I knew Mom and Dad would say Pete was too young to try to start the engine. But I had no choice. I needed his help with the yard.

"Okay," I said. "But you gotta get all your work done first."

He agreed. *"Vrooom, vroom, zoom,"* he sang, spinning his finger through the air.

"Come on, let's eat outside. I wanna get a move-on."

After lunch, Peter gathered up the palm fronds and stacked up the coconuts like cannonballs. He wasn't a lot of help but he was good company. I started the lawn mower and began to cut the grass in the back yard. Our spaniel,

BoBo, ran from the noise and hid in the utility room where we kept the tools and washer and Pete's turtle.

Whenever I mowed the lawn, I imagined my father shaving in the morning. Just as he'd first shave around his mouth and nose, I would mow around the flower beds and trees. And just as he'd quickly shave his cheeks, I would dash back and forth over the open sections of the lawn. And just as he gingerly shaved his neck and up under the dangerous part of his chin, I carefully mowed the steep slope in the back yard down to the canal, afraid I'd slip and plunge into the water with the mower hacking at me.

When I finished, I looked across the yard to see Pete sitting on the back steps, just as my father often looked down to find me sitting on the edge of the bathtub.

I turned off the engine and he came running over.

"Let's play now," he said.

I was ready. I knew Dad wouldn't be home for hours. "Okay, you push the mower to the front yard," I ordered. "I'll get the Zero and meet you in the field."

He was waiting for me when I arrived. "I want you to find a short stick," I said, "so you don't use your finger when you flick the prop."

"Why not?" he asked.

"Just do what I tell you to do. I don't want to have to go find your finger and keep it on ice all the way to the hospital. That would be just a little too gross for me."

While he searched for a stick, I gassed up the plane, flicked the propeller a few times until the engine caught and growled. It was as loud and mean as the lawn mower, or worse, the garbage disposal, which always made me sick to think of it chopping up my hand. It's not the sight of blood which scares me. It's knowing there are no replacement parts for fingers, eyes, ears, feet . . .

Pete ran over. "You promised," he shouted. "You said I could do it."

I turned the engine off. "I was just warming it up. Now, I'll hold the plane and you flick the prop with the stick."

His hand was weak and he couldn't get enough speed on the prop to make the engine start. "Use both hands and give it a good spin."

He did. Finally, the engine started and the propeller chopped at the stick and spit it out to one side. "Go hold the controls," I yelled. When the guide strings were tight I ran with the plane over my head and let it go. The Zero went straight up into the air, then flipped over and came screaming nose-down until it crashed in the sand.

Pete jumped into the air. *"Boom!"* he shouted. "Let's do it again." He ran to get his stick and start the engine.

I could have thrown a bowling ball farther than we got the plane to fly. Each time it left my hands, it jerked up and with all its force blasted straight down into the sand. I couldn't blame the terrible flying on Pete, because I never did any better myself.

"Boom!" he shouted for the last time as the Zero came down on a chunk of concrete and the engine broke away from the fuselage. He looked frightened.

"I'm not mad," I said. "This happens all the time. The screws came loose from all those crashes." I started to repack it into its box. "Besides, we better get back to the yard work."

"I'm tired," Pete whined.

"Just help me a little bit more before Dad gets home," I said. "Or he'll yell at me."

"I want a glass of water," he said and drifted toward the front door.

"Then hurry," I shouted. "I wanna get a move-on."

When he returned, I was the one who was standing still. I was staring almost straight up over my head at the two airplanes. Johnny Foil's biplane was painted bright red and it dashed back and forth over our neighborhood like an enormous trapped bird. Right on its tail was the camera plane, filming Johnny's every stunt. First he made big figure eights. Then he climbed straight up into the air. At the top of his climb, he stood dead-still in the air and fluttered like a kite with his engine sputtering until he started down in tight corkscrew circles. It made me dizzy to watch them.

Pete stood next to me. "Wow," he shouted. "Wow."

I knew Dad was watching through his binoculars. He and his friends were in the radio tower listening to Johnny count out the seconds during each stunt. Dad told me that when you spin down or do loops you have to count out the seconds; otherwise, you might lose track of where you are and crash. So when Johnny does a backward circle he counts, "One thousand one . . . one thousand two . . . one thousand three . . ." and by then the circle should be complete and he knows to steer out of it.

Pete put down the glass of water and raised his finger in the air. *"Bang! Bang! Bang!"* he shouted as Johnny roared by. *"Bang! Bang! Bang!"*

Johnny curved away and circled over our neighborhood as the camera plane followed closely behind. I wished I could fly my Zero with such control.

"Did you see the stars painted on the tail?" I yelled. "Dad painted that."

"I'll shoot it down," he shouted. *"Bang! Bang! Bang!"*

Then Johnny repositioned himself and began to do barrel rolls in big loops from left to right as the camera plane filmed from overhead. I knew from Dad they were "five-second" barrel rolls. "One thousand one . . ." I counted as Johnny began his roll. "One thousand two . . ."

"Bang! Bang! Bang!" shouted Pete, shooting with his finger, and aiming carefully with one eye closed. *"Bang! Bang! Bang!"*

On the count of three, when Johnny was at the highest point of his roll, something happened. I couldn't quite figure it out as I saw a tire flip across the sky. It didn't make sense. Pete kept jumping around with his machine-gun finger. *"Bang! Bang! Bang!"* he blasted. *"Bang! Bang! Bang!"* Another wheel flew through the air, then the camera plane peeled off to the right and swooped away from us. Suddenly, Johnny's engine growled louder than before as his biplane pitched downward like the Zero. *"Bang! Bang! Bang!"* Pete rattled. The plane raced toward the earth. The double wings folded up over the pilot's head with a loud slap and the last I saw of Johnny Foil was just a flag-sized piece of his orange parachute trailing from the cockpit. He hit ground on the other side of the canal from the Peabos' house. We first heard the impact, then the explosion, which was followed by an enormous cloud of fire and oily black smoke.

I was stunned. "What happened?" I asked Pete.

He was crying and hopping from foot to foot. "I didn't mean it," he wailed. "I didn't mean to shoot it down." He spun around and ran into the house with his arms over his head as if he were being chased by bees.

Mom came running from the back yard. She had been in the utility room sorting the wash and still had light clothes over one shoulder and dark clothes over the other. "What happened?" she shouted.

"Johnny's plane crashed," I yelled back. "It went down behind the Peabos' house."

"Oh, God," she cried out. "I better call the airport." She ran toward the front door with the clothes slipping off behind her.

I knew Dad was fine. I didn't know about Johnny. But right now I was worried about Pete.

Mom was still making phone calls when I went inside. She was nervous and attempted to reach Betsy, who was at school, trying out for the ninth-grade cheerleader squad. I could hear the fire trucks racing along the back streets. I opened Pete's bedroom door. The bed was still perfectly made. I checked the closet. Then found him under the bed.

"I didn't mean to do it," he cried as I crawled under.

"But you didn't do anything," I said. "You can't shoot down an airplane with your finger. Don't be a moron."

"Yes, I can," he said. "I just did it."

"No, you can't. Now try and shoot me. Come on."

"No, I'll kill you," he cried.

"Don't be silly," I said. "Come on, get out from under the bed and I'll prove that you can't shoot things down with your finger."

"Don't tell anyone," he begged. "They'll put me in jail."

I knew I could ruin his life at this moment. I could say, "Yes, you shot down an airplane and killed the pilot and they will put you in jail for the rest of your life." But I couldn't be so mean to him.

"I won't tell anyone," I said, "as long as you try and shoot this book with your finger." I set a book on the floor and leaned it against the wall. He aimed his finger at it. *"Bang,"* he whispered. *"Bang, bang."* Nothing happened, but I could tell by his screwy face that he wasn't convinced.

"Now try and shoot things out of the air." I tossed his pillow across the room.

"Bang," he said.

I threw his Godzilla across the room.

"Bang," he said.

I threw his Nerf ball and baseball cap. Each time he shot at them with his finger and each time nothing happened. Then I jumped on him and picked him up and threw him on the bed and rolled him up in the bedspread and sat on him.

"Repeat after me," I demanded. "I can't breathe."

"I can't breathe," said a muffled voice.

"And I can't shoot down planes with my finger."

"I can't shoot down planes with my finger."

"And I'll help Jack with all the yard work for the rest of my life."

"And I'll *never* help Jack again," he shouted and began to twist his way out from under me. He was cured.

Just then, Mom came into the room. "Look what a mess you two have made," she said sharply. But she was crying. "Dad called," she said. Then she turned away to blow her nose into a tissue. "He'll be home soon. Johnny didn't survive." Pete ran over to her and hugged her around the waist.

Dad didn't come home until we were eating dinner. "Sorry I'm so late," he said. "We went over to see his family. They're just stunned."

We watched him scrub his hands at the kitchen sink. "I'm just disgusted," he said bitterly. "The Hollywood guys just flew right into his path. They called it an accident. I call it piss-poor flying. And to make matters worse, somebody stole his wallet. They took it right out of his pocket before anyone arrived."

After dinner I was tired and went to my room. I unlocked my diary but didn't know what to write just yet. I closed my eyes and saw the red biplane buzzing over our house. I kept thinking that maybe the wallet wasn't stolen. Maybe it had been thrown from Johnny's pocket on impact. Maybe it was lost in the bushes far from the plane. I'd find it and fix up the house, have the bugs sprayed and make everything good again. But I was wrong to think this way. It wasn't my money. Instead, I imagined the crash. I felt myself going down. The engine growled and my hands gripped the wheel. The wings folded over my head. My eyes were closed so tight, small explosions of color went off inside my brain before I hit the ground. *"Boom!"* Then I was dead.

I swear this
is true. I was
singing in the
shower and I
was hitting a
high note when
the light bulb
blew out. This
is true. Then
I turned the
shower off.
Then
I
heard
BOB

NITE
HOWLER

BRILLIANT WHIS'
FOUNTAIN

CAUTION
FLAMMABLE
SHOWER
SPARKS

CANDY
ITANI

I WAS SITTING in the Florida room looking out the window, waiting for Johnny Ross and his mother to pick me up for choir practice at the Baptist Mission. My mother is Lutheran and my father is Catholic, but we don't regularly go to church. I had gone with Johnny to the mission a few times when he asked if I'd sing with him on Sundays in the choir. The thought of singing in front of strangers made me nervous. But since this was my family's fifth neighborhood in six years, it was about time I got used to being with strangers. As Betsy always said to me, "Beggars can't be choosers."

Mom was delighted. "Of course you can," she said. "But you'll have to get a haircut and a new white shirt and a bow tie."

I hadn't thought she was going to make such a big deal of it, but I should have known better. Mom loves to watch the Vienna Boys' Choir sing on television. Every Christmas, she decorates the dining-room table with a group of choirboy candles. We even have those giant light-up choirboy statues on our front lawn.

This year, she insisted that I sing in the chorus at school. But I couldn't carry a tune. I was tone deaf and wailed like bagpipes warming up.

"Sing from your diaphragm," Miss Connors would say to me during class, and pat her big belly. "From the diaphragm." She'd play a set of scales on the piano and sing, "Do, re, me, fa, so, la, ti, do."

Then it was my turn. I was great on the first "do, re, me." But when I reached "fa, so, la, ti," my voice splintered like a broken mirror and only a dog could hear my last, painful "doooooough."

"You're singing from the throat," she said, stroking her flabby neck. "Stop straining and sing from the belly." Then she threw her head back and sang the scales as though they were the names of her children. Maybe skinny people can't sing, I thought. All the opera stars were as big as cows . . .

I got up and looked at the clock on my desk. Johnny and his mother were twenty minutes late. I wanted a glass of chocolate milk, but Mom was in the kitchen and I was afraid she was going to tell me for the hundredth time to get a haircut. The back had finally reached the top of my collar, and when I pulled my bangs down really hard, I could tickle my nose. Johnny had long black hair he could comb back in a wave, and I wanted hair just like his. He didn't look like a choirboy. He looked more like a movie star.

"They're here," Mom called.

"Coming," I yelled back. I raced down the hall and through the living room. "Bye."

"Not so fast," she ordered, pointing her finger at my head.

"I'm telling you for the last time that I want you to get a haircut before Sunday."

"I have to run," I said, opening the front door.

"You can either go on your own or I'll have your father take you," she said. "And you know what he'll tell the barber." Dad had been in the navy and he liked haircuts "high and tight." If he had it his way, I'd have to draw hair on my shaved head with a Magic Marker.

"Okay, okay, okay," I moaned and ran out the door.

"Have fun," she called behind me.

The preacher's son, Brent, was in the back seat with Johnny. I didn't know him too well. He went to a special mission school. "Move over," I said, scooting in with them and closing the door.

"Sorry we're late," Johnny said, "but we had to wait for Brent to finish dinner."

"Yeah," said Brent. "Once Dad says grace you can't leave the table till everyone eats everything on their plate, and my sister eats like a snail, so we all have to sit there and watch her."

"Can't you help her?" I asked. "We always make food trades at home."

"Forget it. Dad likes it that she eats slow. It gives him more time to preach at us."

There were two strange things about Brent. The first was that, for a preacher's kid, he said more nasty things about his dad and used more curse words than any other kid I knew. The second was that he was born with six fingers on each hand. But the sixth fingers didn't have a bone in them, so when he moved his hands and spoke, those shriveled fingers danced around like rubber worms.

"You ought to cut those things off," Johnny said, pulling back so they didn't touch him. "They're disgusting."

"Can't," Brent said. "Dad says God gave 'em to me for a good reason and so I have to keep 'em."

"You ought to cut 'em off and use 'em for fishing bait," Johnny said. "I bet you'd catch a shark."

"That's enough, boys," his mother said. I could see her looking hard into the rearview mirror to catch our eyes. "I'm sure Reverend Sears knows what he's talking about. Now you apologize."

But before Johnny could, Brent cut him off. "Mrs. Ross," he twanged, leaning forward and propping his elbows on the back of her seat. "The other day I punched my little sister in the ear and Dad tied my fingers in a knot an' said, 'This is what God gave you these things for, so I can tie your nasty hands together.' "

"It's not nice for a preacher's son to lie," replied Mrs. Ross. "I'm sure he would never do something like that."

I wasn't so sure. Reverend Sears was a big, strong man who was always telling people what to do. He was strict and his sermons were tough. Reverend Sears really got going when it came to people burning in hell. Every week, it seemed like he would give a sermon about another sinner who joined the Hell Hall of Fame. Stealing, lying, cheating, gossiping, cursing, drinking, dancing, and a long, long list of other sins always "bought you a one-way ticket to the Hell Hall of Fame."

"Excuse me, Mrs. Ross," Brent said sweetly. "Do you have a Kleenex?" He crammed one useless finger up his nose and then fake-sneezed. *"Eu,"* he cried, slowly pulling the finger out of his nose. "Look at the booger."

We arrived at the church without another word spoken on the subject. "Call me when you're finished with practice," Mrs. Ross said to Johnny as we got out.

"Will do."

"Thanks for the ride, Mrs. Ross," I said, not wanting her to be annoyed with me.

"Why don't you just kiss her butt goodbye," Brent cracked as she drove off. I didn't say anything back to him, because he was the preacher's son and I didn't know how much trouble he could make for me.

It was my first practice with the choir and I wanted the music director to think I was polite, since once she heard my voice, she'd be sorry I arrived. I had Johnny introduce me. "This is Miss Tate," he said quickly and rejoined Brent. They were trying to rub chewing gum on Becky Earl's new braces.

"It's very nice to meet you, ma'am," I said as clearly as I could. She had big black hair the size of a garden bush piled up on her head and it smelled like lemon furniture polish. It made my eyes water.

"Why, thank you kindly," she said with a heavy Southern accent. "Now, what range do you sing?"

"I'm a tenor," I said.

"You are just what I'm looking for," she chirped. "I have a duet in mind for a tenor and an alto. Oh, this is just splendid. God must have sent you to me."

"Thanks." I knew God did not send me because He knew how rotten my voice was, and soon she would, especially after I shattered a few windows. I just hoped she didn't embarrass me too much. I knew Johnny and Brent were going to gang up on me, and already my heart was beating quickly and my face was hot.

We practiced three songs. I tried to keep my voice low, but she heard me. She canceled the duet. But she was polite enough to have me sing a long, elaborate "Hallelujah," for after the sermon. She no longer thought God sent me, nor did the rest of the choir, who were restless and began to talk while I struggled to sing up and down all those eighth notes. The only luck I had was that Johnny called his mother while I practiced the "Hallelujah" and she was waiting for us when I finished, so we could make a quick getaway.

"Your voice stinks," Brent said to me in the car. "My dad will probably throw you out of the church after he hears that racket."

"Then you sing it," I snapped.

"I won't have time to sing it," he said. "I'll be makin' a fortune sellin' earplugs."

Johnny laughed. "You sound like Tarzan calling the elephants."

"Boys," said Mrs. Ross. "Be nice for a change."

"Drop dead," I said, meaning them, not her.

"That's enough of your back talk, Jack," Mrs. Ross said sharply. Brent took a pen and wrote BUTTHOLE on his hand. "Sniff this," he whispered and rubbed it across my face.

When I woke up the next morning, it was hot and humid. I went out to the kitchen and poured myself a glass of orange juice. Dad was reading the newspaper and Mom was vacuuming the living-room carpet. "This dog hair is driving me nuts," she said. "It's everywhere. I should just vacuum the dog instead of the house."

"That dog needs a haircut," Dad proclaimed without lowering the newspaper.

"You're so right," she said. "I'll call a dog groomer and make an appointment."

"Wait a minute." He jumped to his feet. "There's no

reason to take the dog to a hair salon that charges an arm and a leg when I can do it."

"What do you know about clipping a dog?" she asked.

"I know that it doesn't take a genius to do it. All I need is a pair of clippers."

"Well, I'm not in the mood to argue about it," she said. "Either you do it now or I'm calling the dog barber." She turned the vacuum cleaner on as I retreated down the hall and into the bathroom. All this hair talk was making me nervous. I locked the door and looked into the mirror. Nothing I could do to my hair would make it look shorter. Not even combing it down flat on my head with Vaseline. I decided to wear a baseball cap all day.

Dad returned from the hardware store with a pair of manual hair clippers. He had a wild, determined look on his face. "Bring the dog into the back yard," he ordered.

I cornered BoBo and carried him out back. He looked at me with his big, dumb spaniel eyes that said, "Traitor, traitor, traitor!" Mom arrived with a bucket of soapy water and a towel. "It's BoBo's day of beauty," she remarked. "A haircut and a bath."

Dad stood over BoBo with one leg on either side of him. He leaned forward, grabbed a clump of fur on the back of BoBo's neck, and started to cut. The clippers chewed at the hair. BoBo stood still for about a minute. Then he began to squirm and try to escape. But Dad was possessed. He fell over onto BoBo and the two of them wrestled around in the grass. BoBo yelled and Dad clipped like a madman while calling for me to help hold BoBo down. "Now, don't hurt him," Mom cautioned. "He's scared, he might bite you."

Dad rode him like a rodeo bronco, until he suddenly

jumped up and announced, "There, I'm finished. I told you there's no reason to pay good money to a dog barber when you can do it yourself." He brushed himself off as BoBo sprang to his feet and dashed toward the front yard.

I knew Mom didn't want to hurt Dad's pride or get him angry, so she just picked up the bucket of soapy water and trudged toward the utility room. I followed her with the flea powder. "You know, Mom," I said, "watching Dad just now reminded me that I have to get a haircut today."

She wasn't surprised. "I can't blame you for not wanting to be his next victim," she said. "Take the money out of my wallet and get going."

BoBo followed me to the barbershop. Huge hunks and patches of hair had been cut away unevenly all over his body. He looked a lot like the fairway when Dad plays golf.

I left BoBo outside the barbershop and took my seat in the giant chrome and red-leather chair. I looked into the mirror. With the apron on I looked like a genuine choirboy, which got me thinking about the "Hallelujah." I could feel my throat tighten up into a fist.

My throat was still tight when I woke up the next morning. Mom had a white shirt ironed for me and had bought a yellow-and-red-checked clip-on bow tie.

"I can't wear the bow tie," I whined. "It's ugly. Everyone will laugh at me."

"Don't be nervous just because you have a solo," Mom said. "Nobody will laugh at you."

"They'll be too busy laughing at your voice," snapped Betsy, who had stepped down off her throne and into my room just long enough to be snotty to me. I was doomed.

"You know why they call it a solo?" Betsy cracked again. "Because by the time you finish you'll be all alone."

Johnny's mom picked me up on time. I sat up front with her and let him and Brent have the back seat to themselves. Brent leaned forward and whispered in my ear, "Your head looks like the hair on my old man's butt." I kept my mouth shut. If I'd had a pair of scissors, I'd have clipped his fingers off.

The choir room was just behind the altar in the front of the church. It had its own entrance from the parking lot. We went inside and put on our blue robes. Mine didn't zip up high enough to cover my bow tie. When it was time, we marched out like a jury entering a courtroom and took our places in the pews to the side of the altar.

We sang the first hymn and one of the deacons delivered the first reading. We sang another hymn and a newlywed couple shared the second reading and drove us nuts. He'd start a sentence and she'd finish it. Then he'd start another and she'd finish it.

Reverend Sears was sitting in meditation, heating up for his sermon, when a man in the front pew jumped up and pointed out the window. "A man is runnin' off with the choir pocketbooks," he hollered. "Get him."

Reverend Sears shot up from his chair and dashed out the back door like a rocket. From where I was standing, I watched a thickset man running across the parking lot with all the ladies' purses slung around his neck and shoulders. He must have sneaked in the back door and taken them from the choir changing room. Then I saw Reverend Sears chasing after him. He was a lot faster and tackled the thief from behind. They went down onto the rough asphalt and rolled over and over until a group of church men pulled the thief up onto his feet. They marched him slowly across the parking lot, through the back door, and around to the altar. One of the men used his own necktie to tie the thief's hands behind his back. The deacon brought around the purses and set them on the altar, to the relieved sighs of the choir members.

Then Reverend Sears stood up next to the man and cried out, "What is your name, sinner!"

"Candy Itani," he whispered.

"Louder," demanded Reverend Sears. "And lift your eyes from the floor and face those you have sinned against."

"Candy Itani," he said more loudly and looked out at the congregation. He was bleeding from both his elbows, the knees in his dark trousers were ripped open, and his pink shirt was cloudy with sweat. He was still breathing heavily and trying to wipe the sweat from his eyes onto his round shoulders.

"Now, don't try to run away," said Reverend Sears as he let go of Candy's arm and stepped toward the congregation. "So often I have stood up here and preached that stealing is a sin against God and all mankind," he said, holding the Bible aloft. "I have read passages in the Bible about thieves. We have read about thieves in our newspapers. Some of us have had our homes violated by thieves. They rob us for drugs and alcohol. For gambling and girlfriends. For nice clothes and cars, out of laziness and sloth, and for the sport of stealing, yes . . . even for the sinful pleasure of taking what does not belong to them."

Reverend Sears stopped to catch his breath while the congregation muttered among themselves.

"So tell us, Mr. Itani, since you are a thief, what further sins do you support through your thieving ways?"

Candy Itani stepped toward the choir. "I'm sorry I tried to steal your purses," he said calmly. "I know what I've done is wrong, but I don't have a job and I'm desperate. I need money to feed my family and pay the rent. Like I said, I know what I did was wrong."

"Just knowing isn't good enough," Reverend Sears interrupted. "As Christians we can forgive you, and we do forgive you. We pray for your family and ask that you provide for them with honest work. And we invite you to join our church. Instead of stealing our money, you can add to our prayers."

Maybe I was wrong about Reverend Sears. I thought then that he would let Candy Itani go and we would take up a collection to help him feed his family. It would be a lot better than taking up a collection to put another missionary out in the Amazon.

"But we are not to sit in judgment of you," continued Reverend Sears. "God has laws and society has laws, Mr. Itani. You have broken those laws . . . Mr. Ross," he said gravely, pointing to Johnny's father, "go call the police. Not only has this man earned a one-way ticket to hell, but he's going to prison along the way."

The organ started up and I recognized the lead-in for the "Hallelujah." Miss Tate gave me an intense look and we both stood up as planned. I felt nervous, but after watching how frantic Candy was, how ashamed he was, sweating and apologizing to us all, I didn't care what people thought of my voice. I sang with my eyes closed so I couldn't see the congregation or the choir director. I listened to the music and sang, trying to lift my voice along the notes. I slurred across all the high notes, peaked like a car crash, and dried up on the low notes. I sang loud and I breathed deep and let out the great relief of that long "Hallelujah."

"Amen," shouted a woman in the front. "Amen."

I smiled and felt proud of myself.

"Pee-ew," Johnny whispered.

You brown-nosing suck-up, I thought to myself. If Brent's the kind of friend you want, then you can have him.

Everyone could hear the police sirens, and as they grew louder I knew they were coming for Mr. Itani. He knew it, too. He looked over his shoulder toward the back door. His body jerked in that direction, but by then a group of men had him by the arms.

The police marched up the center aisle as if they were getting married. They handcuffed Candy Itani and led him away.

"I think he's pissed his pants," Johnny remarked and pointed. "You can see it runnin' down his leg."

"I can't believe Dad invited him to come back," Brent said. "They oughta lock him up and throw away the key."

I sat there and hated myself for not telling them both to go take a one-way trip to the Hell Hall of Fame.

After church I usually ate lunch at Johnny's house, but today I asked Mr. Ross to take me straight home. "I don't feel well," I said, sounding hollow. I sat in the car and made up my mind never to go back to that church again. I figured I would have to see Johnny in school the next day, but if he didn't say anything to me, I wouldn't say anything to him.

When I got home, I told Mom that I didn't want to go anymore. She asked why and I told her what had happened.

"Then you don't have to go," she said. "Besides, I've been thinking that we'll all start back at the Lutheran church." But I knew we wouldn't. And I knew my friendship with Johnny would dry up.

seen the mo
a "Mockingbird"
really ratty do
rabies. atti
I have a
her) came
and sho
If this

RABIES

I HAD BEEN READING a lot of detective novels. Dad likes to read books about World War II. Betsy reads a lot of "English literature," as she calls it. Mom reads short stories, and Pete reads picture books. I had been reading so many detective books I began to think I was a detective myself.

"Hey, Dad, can I find anything for you?"

"A new job," he said, turning a page. I wasn't that good. He had gone through five jobs in five years.

"What about you, Mom?"

"I lost an earring," she said, without looking up.

I went right to work. First, I searched where she said she'd last seen it. Nothing. So then I followed a hunch. Mom has glasses, but she doesn't wear them. She doesn't like the heavy way they feel on her nose. So when she vacuums around the house she picks up things she can't see. Once she vacuumed part of my stamp collection off my desk. So I checked the vacuum-cleaner bag and, sure enough, found the earring, twenty-eight cents, and the tiny silver key to Betsy's diary.

When I asked Betsy if I could find something for her, she said, "You should go find something worth doing."

"I need money," I whispered in her ear. "How much would you pay for the key to your diary?"

"I'll murder you in your sleep," she said. But I didn't care if she wanted to kill me. My days as a detective were numbered. I had rabies.

Four days earlier, I had been bitten by a dog. I'd left my Raleigh bike outside the library, and when I came out, a boy about my age and a big black dog were standing next to it. Dad had bought me the Raleigh three years ago for Christmas. It was red with chrome fenders, a chrome headlight and bell, and a basket on either side of the rear wheel. It was an expensive English bike and Dad had bought it back when we had money. But now there wasn't any extra money to afford "special things," as Mom put it. I had never seen another bike like it, and a lot of people stopped to admire it.

As I lifted the kickstand with my foot the dog began to growl. I swung my leg over the seat and the dog jumped at me and bit me on the ankle. I jerked my leg back and lost my balance. I fell over sideways, with the bike crashing down on top of me. I had a stack of books in my backpack and they dug into my ribs when I hit the sidewalk. The dog lunged at my face.

"Hold him back," I shouted, but the boy didn't move to call off the dog. He looked directly into my eyes and did nothing.

"Get it away from me," I yelled. He turned and walked

away. "Hey! Come back here," I hollered. Maybe it's not his dog, I thought. The dog went back down to my ankle. I tried to crawl farther under the bike to protect myself. But it clamped its teeth on my leg and tried to drag me away. It wanted to bury me like a bone in its back yard. I yanked my leg back and kicked it in the face. Suddenly, it lost interest in me and ran after the boy as if nothing had ever happened. I saw the boy pet the dog on the head and then reach into his pocket and toss him a biscuit.

I stood up and walked my bike around the building. I wasn't hurt and my bike was okay, but I was mad. I rolled down my sock and looked at the two bites. They weren't bleeding, but the skin was broken in three places. I knew a kid who'd been bitten by a raccoon and had to have forty rabies shots in his stomach. Every afternoon for a month the school nurse came into the classroom and escorted him down the hall to the clinic. A half hour later he staggered back to his seat as if he'd been punched in the belly. The teacher let him rest his head on her stuffed Piglet.

One day, she asked us a math question and he raised his hand. "You must be feeling better," she remarked. He threw up on her shoes.

I didn't want forty shots in the stomach with a needle as thick and long as a pencil. But in case I got rabies, I needed to know where the dog lived. If I started foaming at the mouth and biting everyone I could tell Dad who to sue.

So I'd followed the boy up the street. I didn't want to get close because I was afraid the dog might bite me again. After five blocks, he turned onto Cactus Street and went into a small wooden house at number 1227.

•

"Five dollars for the diary key," I said to Betsy.

"Two," she replied. I followed her to her room. She closed the door and grabbed me around the neck. "Give it to me, you jerk."

"I'll bite you," I managed to say. "I have rabies."

She let me go. "You're gross! Now, give it to me."

"A dollar," I said. She gave me a quarter. I gave her the key. She kicked me in the leg and I dropped to the floor.

"They shoot people with rabies," she growled. "I hope I get to pull the trigger."

I thought I'd go to the library and check out more detective novels. Our school was too cheap to have its own library. A Broward County Book Mobile arrived every Friday and class by class we took turns checking out books. But they didn't have many detective novels. Mostly they had smelly old books that had other people's names or library seals stamped on the title page. There were a lot of books on subjects like canning vegetables and how to get soup stains out of silk ties. I hate having to read books that other people think are junk. "Something is better than nothing," said Mrs. Marshall when I complained. But reading junk books is the same as having to eat someone else's leftovers.

Instead of going straight to the library, I rode my bike over to a field of thick bushes across the road from Gus's Gas Station. I was always curious about Gus's Gas Station because there were no other stations in Fort Lauderdale named after a person. We had fancy Exxon and Chevron and Texaco stations, but there was only one greasy station named after Gus. In the detective books, the most clever criminals always had their hideouts in fake businesses. I had been spying on Gus from across the road, trying to catch him and his gang doing criminal things like stuffing bodies into oil drums so they could dump them out in the ocean. Maybe they were secret agents and the giant gas tank under the station was a spy headquarters and the light pole was a radio antenna.

Whenever I was riding with Dad, I asked him to stop and buy gas at Gus's. But he wouldn't.

"He sells cheap gas," Dad said. "People say he puts water in it."

"Is that all?"

"That's bad enough," Dad replied.

As I crouched behind a bush and watched, nothing unusual happened at Gus's except for the normal stuff that would happen at any gas station. People pulled up in their cars and Gus hobbled out of his office and put gas in their tanks and washed their windshields. I didn't see anything like secret signals, or secret doors, or wanted criminals hiding behind all the used tires in his garage. He didn't even go near a water hose, or drink a glass of water. Between customers he just sat in his office and peeled an apple with a knife big enough to amputate my leg.

I got back on my bike and rode down Federal Highway. I passed by the parking lot at King's Department Store. A carnival had set up in the parking lot. "Live a little," I said to myself. "You'll soon be a goner." I parked the bike and ran to buy a ticket to the WILD ROCKET. A sign said it was the most powerful ride in the world. It was built like a cigar, with a seat in a little cage on each end. An axle ran through the middle of the cigar, and when the ROCKET spun around, it went about a hundred miles an hour. There was another sign that read: "Warning! This ride is not safe for people with heart problems." It didn't say anything about rabies.

I climbed into my cockpit and put on my seat belt. I made

sure my shoelaces were tied so my shoes wouldn't come off during the ride and hit me in the head. Suddenly, the engine started and I grabbed the handlebar. In a minute I couldn't even keep my eyes open and I screamed bloody murder. Then I felt like I passed out.

When the ride stopped, a carnival worker opened my cage and unlocked my seat belt. He gave me a hand and helped me down. The world was still spinning at a hundred miles per hour. When my feet hit the ground, I stumbled forward and fell. My blood felt like Coca-Cola when you shake it up. I crawled and staggered around the parking lot until I found a light pole to lean against. I wiped my mouth on my sleeve. It was all foamy. The first sign of rabies. It was starting. My leg began to throb.

To hell with the library, I thought. I've got to save myself. I turned onto Cactus Street and pedaled as hard as I could. I needed to see the dog. Because if it was still alive and not foaming at the mouth, I'd live. But as I sped by I didn't see the dog. Instead, I saw that the front door was wide open and an old beat-up couch was out on the sidewalk, along with a few cardboard boxes of junk. It all looked suspicious to me.

There were no curtains on the windows and suddenly it struck me that they had moved. "Oh, crap," I said. They probably knew their dog had rabies and that I was infected and so they had to get out of town before I died and they were arrested for murder. I slowed down and circled back to the house. Even though I was afraid of the dog I stopped in their front yard and got off my bike. I walked up to the open door and knocked on it. "Hello?" I shouted. "Anybody home?" If anyone answered, I planned to ask if my friend Frankie Pagoda lived there. But there was no answer.

"Anybody home?" I yelled again. There was no answer. My ankle began to throb. Soon I'd be foaming at the mouth, running on my hands and feet, and biting the neighbors. Finally I'd be tracked down and captured by police dogs, but it would be too late to save me. I'd be shot and buried in a pet cemetery.

I limped over to the boxes of junk on the front lawn and began to search through them. I needed their names, and if I was lucky, I'd get their new address so I could find out if their dog was infected. The boxes were mostly filled with broken stuff: a chipped plate, a used toothbrush, old shoes, ripped shirts, an old Halloween mask of Spider-Man, and a broken thermos bottle. But there were a few old letters. I shoved them into my backpack. I felt really guilty going through someone's garbage, especially in the middle of the day. Real detectives always did this stuff at night when no one was looking. Plus, I knew I'd have to hide all the stuff from my mom because she really disliked "snoops and sneaks," and if she caught me, she'd probably turn me in to the police.

"Hey, kid," a man hollered from next door.

I jumped up and spun around. "What?"

"Why are you going through their trash?" he asked. He was big. Maybe an off-duty cop.

"I'm looking for used books," I replied. "For our school library."

"Don't you know there's a hurricane heading our way?" He took a couple steps toward me.

"No," I said and trotted over to my bike.

"Well, you better get a move-on. That hurricane should hit the shore in a few hours."

"Thanks," I said.

The wind had already picked up. I hopped on my bike and flew down the street. During hurricane season it was pretty normal to have a lot of warnings. Just about everyone kept a hurricane-tracking map in their house and charted the movement of the latest hurricane, so they'd know if it was heading our way. But the hurricanes were unpredictable and would veer off in all directions. Nobody knew if it was really going to hit until it was actually on top of us. The best part about hurricanes was that we were always being let out of school early to go help our parents, who had gotten out of work early, to tape up the windows and tie down everything around the house that could easily be blown away.

By the time I rode up our driveway, Dad was nailing sheets of plywood over the floor-to-ceiling windows in the Florida room.

"Where've you been?" he yelled. The words seemed to blow up over his head and away. I parked my bike in the carport and went to help him. I couldn't tell him I was spying on a dog who gave me rabies. And I didn't want to tell him I was at the carnival having fun while he was working his butt off. "I was spying on Gus," I yelled back and held up one end of the plywood.

"What were you bothering him for?"

"You said he puts water in his gas tanks, and I wanted to catch him."

"You knucklehead," he said. "He wouldn't do it in broad daylight. He'd wait until it was dark."

"Well, I thought with the hurricane coming on, he might try something."

"Well, think about doing the right thing and sticking

around the house when you're needed," he said. He pounded another nail through the plywood and stopped yelling.

While Dad and I finished the windows, Mom and Betsy took care of the other hurricane-emergency procedures we were taught on television. They filled plastic jugs with drinking water, turned up the refrigerator to get it real cold because the electricity always goes off, put candles and matches in all the rooms, and checked the batteries in the flashlights and radios. Dad had Pete put the rake and hose and lawn tools in the utility room. I got the aluminum ladder for Dad and held it as he climbed up to the roof to remove the television antenna. When he came down, he said to me, "Make sure you put your bike in the utility room so it doesn't blow around."

"In a minute," I said. I put the ladder away, then set up some weather experiments. In science class we saw a movie on the weird power of hurricanes and tornadoes. It showed how high winds had driven plastic drinking straws through trees. I thought that was pretty cool so I went into the kitchen and got some straws. I stripped the paper off and set them out on a tree stump. I aimed them for our plywood shutters, thinking that if I was lucky they would stick in the wood like darts. Next, I had an army man with a plastic parachute. I took a marker and wrote my name and telephone number and "Reward offered for return" on the parachute, then threw it on top of the carport so it might get a flying start when the winds picked up. My last experiment was sort of dangerous but I did it anyway. Dad had some steel rods in the utility room. I took one out and sunk it into the ground by the edge of the canal. It stuck out about two feet above the ground. I was hoping it would conduct lightning and melt. When I passed through the front yard, Dad was snipping the coconuts out of the palm trees with a long tree clipper.

"I've seen these things fly through the air like cannonballs," he yelled.

All the excitement was great. Ever since I had read about the adventures of the Swiss Family Robinson, I wanted our family to be like them. My greatest wish come true would have our family carried away by a huge tidal wave and washed up on a deserted island where we had to build our own house in the trees and grow our own food and ride wild horses and educate one another.

"Did you put your bike away?" Dad asked.

"I forgot," I said.

"Well, go toss these coconuts in the canal, and then put it away like I told you."

"Okay," I said and loaded up my arms.

After I had thrown the coconuts into the water, Mom called to me. "Hurry up and get inside," she yelled. "I want you to take a shower before I fill the tub with water."

When I was undressing I reexamined my dog bite. The teeth marks were still red and swollen, and when I touched them, they throbbed. Rabies, I thought. I should tell Mom and Dad right now so they still have time to take me to the hospital. But what if it's not rabies? What if we dash to the hospital and the doctor says it's just a simple dog bite and then the hurricane gets worse and we are stuck at the hospital? Everyone will hate me for being a big baby. Dad will roll his eyes. Mom will try to be nice. Betsy will treat me like a moron, and Pete will laugh until he falls over. I decided not to tell them. It was a chance I'd have to take.

I went into my bedroom and locked the door. I turned my crummy radio on to the hurricane-watch station and began to go through the letters I had found at Cactus Street. I was in luck. Their names were Mrs. Cleo Stone and Jimmy Stone. There didn't seem to be a Mr. Stone. I had an old electric bill, a postcard sent to Jimmy from someone named Harry, a bill-collection notice for late rent, a contest application, a church-picnic notice, and a telephone bill.

I wrote their old phone number on a scrap of paper and went into Mom and Dad's bedroom. They were in the living room watching the hurricane report on the one television station we could still get. I dialed the number and got what I'd hoped for. A tape-recorded message from the phone company announced: "The number you have reached has been changed to 723-4423."

I quickly rehearsed my thoughts and dialed the new number.

"Hello," answered a boy.

"Is this Jimmy Stone?" I asked in an adult voice.

"Yes."

"This is the dog pound," I said. "We're calling to make sure your dog is properly locked up during the hurricane."

"Have you seen my dog?" he asked excitedly. "He ran away and we've been searching for him everywhere." Then he yelled away from the phone, "Hey, Mom. It's the dog pound looking for Peanut."

"Give me the phone," a woman said.

I hung up. Then I ran back to my room and peeled off my sock. My ankle was pounding. The bruises looked dark and infected. I squeezed around a puncture and some watery pus dribbled out. I'm a dead man, I thought. Jimmy Stone's dog had gone mad and run away.

I removed my diary from under my mattress. I unlocked it and wrote: "My Last Will and Testament. Everything I own goes to Pete." I signed my name to make it official. Then I spit on the page. Under it I wrote, "This is what killed me!"

All evening long we sat in the living room and watched disaster movies on television. First we watched *Key Largo,* where a hurricane wipes out a hotel in the Florida Keys. That was followed by *The Poseidon Adventure,* which showed an ocean liner flipped over by a tidal wave. Then *Earthquake* came on and we watched a city crumble and burn. All the disaster scenes seemed real because of the hurricane winds howling around our house and the rain beating against the plywood shutters. I thought up a movie where a boy gets rabies and bites everyone in the whole town and infects them and then they begin to spread out across the entire country and the President has to call out the army to shoot all the rabid fiends. But the rabid people chew up the army and the President has to decide to drop the atomic bomb on the dog people. It could be the end of civilization.

"You look like you've seen a ghost," Mom said, running her hand over my head. "Don't worry, the house won't blow away."

"I'm fine," I replied. I had only two choices now. I could just go find a safe place to die, or I could get forty shots in my stomach and throw up every day. I'd rather die.

We were watching *King Kong* when the electricity went off.

"Okay, the party's over," said Dad. "Time for bed."

Pete had already fallen asleep, and Mom carried him up the hallway to his room. I was tired and fell asleep right away. I slept through the rest of the hurricane and didn't wake up until Dad pushed open my bedroom door and yelled at me. "Jack! Get up this instant!" Even before I opened my eyes I knew he was furious. What did I do? Did I bite everyone in my sleep? My heart was pounding.

"Get out here!" he hollered. What kind of trouble was I in? I ran down the hall and out the front door. Dad was lying on his back, half under his truck, trying to pull something out from around the back axle. I stood by his feet as he wrestled with a bunch of tangled pipes. Then suddenly he got it free and pushed it toward me. It was my Raleigh bike, all twisted up like a pretzel.

"Didn't I tell you to put your bike away!" he shouted.

I started to cry.

"Well?" he asked. "I'm waiting."

"You did."

"Now look at it," he said. "It's ruined. You just don't listen to me. How do you expect to learn anything if you don't listen?"

I looked down at the bike. Every inch of it was bent. It must have blown under the truck, and when he pulled out of the carport, it got curled up under the wheels.

"How do you expect to get good things if you can't take care of them?" Dad continued. "You know we don't have money to burn." I knew this speech and it made me sad for everyone in our family. We just didn't have the money we once had. When Dad's good watch stopped running, he'd bought a cheap Timex. We'd bought a used black-and-white television when our color set gave out. We didn't even have a car of our own. Dad had the company truck, which I'd just about ruined.

"I'm sorry," I said to him.

"I'm sorry, too," he said, but he was still mad. He got in the truck and drove off.

I guess I don't need a bike anyway, I thought. I'll be dead soon.

I got dressed and started to work around the house like the madman I was. I picked up all the fallen tree limbs, cut them up with a hatchet, and piled them by the side of the road for the garbage truck. I raked the lawn and swept the sidewalk and driveway. I wanted to take down the plywood shutters and have the house in perfect shape for Dad's return, but Mom said they were too heavy. "What else can I do, then?" I asked her.

"If you're all caught up," she said, "you're free until your dad gets home."

"Okay." I ran around to the back of the house and checked on my experiments. I couldn't find the plastic drinking straws anywhere. I found my parachute soldier tangled up in a bush by the side of the house, and lightning had not struck the steel rod by the canal. I pulled it out and put it back in the utility room. That's when I saw Pete's new bike and got an idea.

I went into the house and knocked on his bedroom door. "Pete," I whispered.

"Yes," he said.

"Can you keep a secret?"

"Yeah, what?" he asked.

"I have something important to tell you." I slipped into his room and locked the door behind me. "Cross your heart you won't tell."

"Cross my heart," he repeated.

"Then look at this." I kicked off my tennis shoe and rolled

down my sock. The bite marks were still red and puffy. "I got bit by a dog last week and now I have rabies," I said. "And I think I'm going to die."

Immediately, he started to cry.

"Don't cry," I whispered. "I think you can save me."

"How?" he asked, sniffing and wiping his nose.

"Loan me your bike. I think I know where the dog lives who bit me. If I can find it, then I'll know for sure if I have rabies." It was a new birthday bike and I knew he didn't want to loan it to me. Especially after he saw what happened to my bike. But I was desperate. "Am I foaming at the mouth yet?" I asked him. I smacked my lips together and let some drool run out of the corner of my mouth and onto my chin.

He looked at me with fear. "I don't think so," he said shakily. "You're only drooling."

"That's the first sign," I moaned. "Just make sure I don't bite you." I rolled my sock back up and put on my shoe. "Will you loan it to me? As you can see, it's a matter of life or death."

"Okay," he said. "But don't tell Dad."

"I'll be back before he comes home from work," I said.

I had a theory. I had read a book called *The Incredible Journey*, which was about a family who had moved across the country without their pets and the story was about how the pets had to track them three thousand miles to find them. I figured that the dog may have gotten confused by the move and returned to the old house.

I took Jimmy Stone's telephone number and a couple of dollars in change I had taped into my diary. My first stop was the grocery store. I went to the pet-food section and picked out a box of dog bones to keep Peanut from chewing on me if I found him. Then I rode to 1227 Cactus Street. Their old house had been kicked around by the hurricane. The windows on the east side were blown in. The door was open, and even from the sidewalk I could see water and glass on the living-room floor. The boxes of trash I had found yesterday were no longer on the front lawn. Everything had blown away. Up and down the street people were clearing debris from their lawns and raking up all the branches and leaves. I looked around to see if there were any interesting disasters. Once, after Hurricane Cleo, I had seen a canoe balanced on the roof of a house, and a tree that had crushed a station wagon. But everything on Cactus Street looked pretty normal, so I had nothing to do but enter the house and look for Peanut. I opened the box of dog bones and walked up the sidewalk. "Here, Peanut," I called out and tossed a dog bone into the empty living room. It landed with a splash. "Here, Peanut," I called from the front door and threw another bone. "Come and get it."

I took a step into the house. Now I am trespassing, I thought, and if I'm bit by a mad dog everyone will say it's my own fault, especially my dad, who will probably say something like, "Didn't I tell you never to enter a stranger's house where a mad dog is hiding?"

The water was an inch deep in the living room. I could feel the same fear run through me that I had felt when the dog bit me. "Here, Peanut," I said and threw a dog bone down the dark hallway. "Good Peanut," I called. The first door I reached was on my right. I opened it just a crack and peeked in. It was the bathroom. "Peanut," I whispered. I slipped a dog bone through the crack. As my eyes grew accustomed to the dark, I saw three more doors. The first one was open. I tiptoed to the edge of the opening and peeked in. "Here, Peanut," I said. But there was no Peanut. I took a deep breath and tried to walk quietly to the next closed door. My tennis shoes squeaked on the wet floor. I knocked. "Are you in there, Peanut?" I opened the door and threw in a dog bone. He wasn't there. There was only one more door and it was open. I peeked into the room. "Peanut? Are you in here?" I threw a dog bone in the dark corner of the room. Then something in the room's closet stirred. My heart jumped. I knew the sound of a dog's nails clacking on the concrete floor. I wanted to run, but I had to see if it was Peanut and if he was foaming at the mouth. I threw a handful of dog bones at the closet door. He barked. "Peanut, come out," I shouted. I threw another bone toward the closet. Then I grabbed the door handle and began to back out of the room. "Peanut, come out," I called. He barked once more, then lunged out of the closet. The floor was wet and he slid in a panic across the room. I screamed and pulled the door shut.

But I had to open it again. I peeked in. "Come here, Peanut," I said. "It's okay." He turned and looked at me. I threw him a dog bone. Even if he jumped at me I had time to yank the door shut before he reached me. He looked at me and barked a few times and I threw him some more dog bones. If he eats, I thought, he isn't rabid. I knew that sick animals never ate. He barked again, then sniffed at a dog bone and started to chew it. I didn't see any foam around his mouth. I threw him another bone and he pawed at it while he chewed another. He seemed really hungry. I opened the door and slowly walked toward him. "Good Peanut," I said. "Good dog." I held a bone out to him and he took it in his mouth as I pet him on his head and scratched his ears. "You dumb dog," I said. "You went home to the wrong house."

I dumped the box of bones on the floor then walked out of the room, closing the door behind me. I didn't have rabies! I didn't have to die or go mad or bite my family to death. I ran down the sidewalk and hopped on Pete's bike. There was a pay telephone at Gus's Gas Station and I rode over there as fast as I could. The gas station was closed for business. A big sign was propped against the gas pump: CLOSED—WATER IN GAS TANK DUE TO HURRICANE. Darn, I thought. Now I'll never know if he put the water in himself. I could just hear Dad saying that Gus was using the hurricane as a cover-up now that everyone was wise to him selling watered-down gas.

The pay phone was on the outside of the building. I put in the dime and dialed Jimmy Stone's number.

"Hello," he answered.

"Is this Jimmy Stone?" I asked in my adult voice.

"Yes," he said.

"This is the city dog pound, and we've found your dog in the back bedroom at 1227 Cactus Street."

"Oh, that's great," he cried. "Hey, Mom," he yelled. "They found Peanut at our old house."

"Let me have the phone," she said.

Oh no! I slammed down the phone. I stood still for a minute. Then suddenly I shouted, *"Case closed!"*

I feel like a zombie in love. The only thing that can save me from being a zombie is her kiss. But I'll be a zombie anyway if Mrs. Marshall sees what I've done to my desk. I found a nail and scratched her name heart o Then I heart o name dre both Then I d blood. The the room.

DONNA LOWRY

"LOOK OUT. There's gonna be a fight," Gary Rook hollered. I looked up and saw his sister's big pink Ford pull into their driveway.

We were in his wide back yard, shooting arrows at a scarecrow his dad had planted in their vegetable garden. We had sawed off the steel points and twisted used thread spools onto the ends. When we missed the scarecrow, we didn't want to kill old Mrs. Gibbons on her back porch.

Gary was allowed to do almost anything he wanted to do. His dad worked all day building fancy doghouses for a chain of kennel clubs, and his mother sat in the house and read gossip magazines and watched soap operas. Last month, Gary rode their riding lawn mower to the grocery store just to buy a Royal Crown Cola. He cut through a lot of lawns and left a path to the store and back. When people called his house to complain, his mom told them all to drop dead.

His sister had moved out of the house last month.

"Mom just found out that Angela's living with a divorced *mountain man,*" Gary said. "And she's mad as all get-out."

They were from Tennessee. I imagined a scrawny man wearing a coonskin cap.

I heard the front door slam.

"You have no right telling me how to live my life," shouted Angela. "It's my life and I can do as I please."

"If you lived decently I wouldn't have to tell you how to live," Mrs. Rook hollered.

"It's not right for you to phone me up at all hours of the day and night and call me names," Angela shouted.

"I wouldn't have to call you names if you'd just run your life like I brought you up to live it," Mrs. Rook yelled.

I didn't like hearing Mom and Dad argue, and now I felt the same way just listening to Gary's mom and sister. But Gary snuck across the ground and knelt under the kitchen window so he could hear better.

I looked at my watch. It was four o'clock and time to go home. Mom had taken a job as a bank teller at First Federal Savings and Loan and wanted us cleaned up for dinner when she arrived from work.

Finally, Angela yelled out louder than before, "You drive me crazy."

"I just wish I could drive you to your senses." The door slammed shut and Angela started up her car with a roar. Her tires squealed in the driveway and just when I thought she was driving off, she suddenly turned the car and started driving on the grass. She drove up over the low azalea hedge into the back yard. The engine roared and grass and dirt kicked out behind the rear tires. I froze. She drove right by me, then between Gary's house and the Gibbonses'. Then I saw her circling back toward us again, only this time faster. I ran for a big palm tree. Gary stayed pressed up against the back of the house. Mrs. Rook was yelling out the back door. The pink car skidded sideways across the grass while Angela spun the steering wheel one way and then another. Her face was puckered up around her mouth and her wig had slipped over to one side, making her head look huge and uneven. I kept running. Angela lost control of the car. She looped around in a circle and plowed across the vegetable garden, flattening the scarecrow. The engine stalled and I heard her laughing as I sprinted for the street.

She started up and fishtailed around to her front yard. When she reached the street, her tires jerked and squealed and I smelled the burnt rubber as the car took a hard left and was gone.

I ran toward home. I cut across the Veluccis' yard, jumped a hedge, jumped a flower bed, and ran around a wading pool to our back door. I whipped it open, ran down the hall and into my bedroom. My heart was pounding and I was panting like a dog.

When I caught my breath, I pulled out my diary. "I wish I was a cop," I wrote. "I'd arrest Gary's sister for attempted murder! There ought to be a law against people like her driving cars." I squeezed the book closed over a plastic sample packet of cologne I took from Betsy's fashion magazine. It popped open like a blood blister. The smell was horrid, like hospital air. The people who make this junk should also be arrested, I thought.

I began thinking about Donna Lowry because she wore perfume. But when I smelled hers, it made my shoulders shiver. She had long, reddish-brown hair. She wore blue jeans and T-shirts and white sneakers to school. She was smart and popular and a member of the Safety Patrol. Only six kids could be members of the Safety Patrol and everyone thought they were the coolest kids in the class. They got silver badges on a bright orange belt that made an X across their chests. They had traffic-police whistles and could stop cars to help kids cross the streets leading to school. And if cars wouldn't stop they could write down their license-plate number and report them to the police. I wanted to join. I could meet Donna and maybe I could arrest Gary's sister.

Donna's Safety Patrol location was the farthest away from school. There were few houses around that part of Lloyd Estates. Most of the land had been bulldozed over into fields of sand and fast-growing saw grass. On her corner was an old house trailer almost overgrown with flowering bushes and low trees. I didn't normally pass her post on my way to school, but every day for the last month I'd gone out of my way. She had a giant tin policeman on wheels that she pushed into the middle of the road each morning. He held a big STOP sign in one hand. Donna stood next to him and directed traffic. She was a real pro. A chrome whistle was jammed into the corner of her mouth and her hair was tucked under a blue baseball cap. When the wind was just right I thought I smelled her perfume. White Shoulders.

One morning when I arrived, she was dragging the policeman across the scrubby field. I always tried to think of something interesting to say when I saw her but never did better than "Good morning" or "Hi" or "See you around." This was my chance.

"Need any help?" I hollered.

"Yeah."

I ditched my new bike. It was a three-speed girl's model Dad had gotten for me at a yard sale. I ran over and grabbed one of the tin man's arms. We dragged him to the road.

"Every damn morning I have to get up extra early just to drag this cop out of the field," she said angrily. "Some jerks keep dragging it away in the night and I have to find it. I'm beginning to hate this job."

"Why do you do it?" I asked.

"Because I wanna be a cop when I grow up. My dad's a cop and my uncle's a detective."

"I don't know if I want to be a cop," I said, "but I'd like to arrest people."

"Then you should join the Safety Patrol. You get a real police badge and you can make a citizen's arrest on people who don't do what you tell 'em to do." She looked at her watch. "Hey, you better get going," she said, and smiled at me. "I don't want to have to arrest you for being late."

I got on my bike. "See you later," I sang and waved goodbye. I was so excited. I just knew everything was going to work out for me and Donna. I hadn't had a girlfriend since third grade, when I threw myself out of a tree in front of Melissa Foster and landed on my back. She took pity on me for about a week, then got tired of my tricks.

After school, I stayed behind and waited for everyone to leave before I approached Mrs. Marshall.

"Yes," she said as she tidied up her desk. "What is it?"

"I'd like to join the Safety Patrol," I said. "I think I'd be good at it."

"Have you done this before?" she asked.

"No," I replied.

"Well," she said, opening her bottom desk drawer. "You're in luck today. Donna quit at lunchtime and you can take her place."

Quit! That can't be right. I wanted to step back and say, "Well, forget it," but didn't have the guts.

She handed me the badge, whistle, and orange belt. "You'll be on Donna's old corner. Do you know where that is?"

"Yes, ma'am," I replied. "I pass by it every day."

"Fine," she said. "I expect you to be kind and courteous. And one more thing. Make sure you wheel the tin policeman into the middle of the road when you begin and put it to the side of the road when you finish."

As she rattled on, I got up enough nerve to ask, "Why did Donna quit?"

"Personal reasons," Mrs. Marshall replied. "She said someone had been bugging her every morning."

I didn't say another word. *Bugging her?* Is that what she thinks of me? I got on my bike and raced home. I wondered if I could quit, but then Donna would know I only joined to be her boyfriend. I was stuck. *Bugging her! Bugging her!* It made my head pulse each time I said the words to myself.

When I got home I tried on my cop outfit and told Betsy about my new job.

"You know where they get those tin policemen?" she asked. I didn't. "They're Safety Patrolmen who've been flattened by maniac drivers."

"Leave me alone," I yelled, but an image of Gary's insane sister flashed across my mind.

"My pleasure," Betsy replied.

I went into my room and unlocked my diary. It smelled

like an old lady's hankie. "Donna hates me," I wrote. "The moment I joined she quit because I've been *bugging her* every morning. She thinks I'm some kind of nut like the losers who call in to the lonely hearts radio show and beg people to be nice to them."

I got up extra early the next morning and put on my orange Safety Patrol belt and my badge and hung the whistle around my neck. Then I got on my bike and rode down to my corner.

The tin policeman was nowhere in sight. I walked through the field until I found him knocked over onto his face. Someone had thrown rocks at him and he was all dented up and his arm was twisted back. It looked as if he was playing ping-pong. "Come on," I said with a sigh. I jerked him up under his arms, dragged him across the field, and stood him in the middle of the street.

I checked my watch. I had a half hour on duty and then I had to return to school. A few kids came by, but since there were no cars coming, I didn't get to jump out into the street and make a car come to a screeching halt. I just waved the kids across.

Then I saw Donna riding up on her bike. I figured she was coming by to laugh at me.

"I wanted to see how you were doing," she said.

"Okay, once I found the policeman. Mrs. Marshall told me you quit."

"What really got to me," Donna said, "was the old lady in the trailer." She picked up a rock and threw it into the bushes alongside the trailer. "That old lady drives me nuts. She's always calling me to help her lift something or reach something or get her something from the store. I'm a cop, not a nurse. She should be arrested and locked up in a nursing home. You'll see." She hopped on her bike and rode off. "Whatever you do, *don't* help her," she shouted.

"Yes! Yes! Yes!" I sang as she turned a corner. "She doesn't hate me. She hates someone else!"

When it was time, I hid the policeman in the bushes to the side of the house trailer and rode to school. Mrs. Marshall hadn't even started her copying frenzy yet.

The next morning, I woke up humming another stupid song from *The Sound of Music*. That movie was still driving me crazy. I put on my rust-colored slacks, green shirt, and brown socks. As I buckled my Safety Patrol belt, I thought I might go to the drive-in theater and try to arrest the owner, "for crimes against my ears." Then I could lock him in a little room and play that movie a million times in a row until he went *insane* . . .

When I arrived on my corner I found my tin policeman just where I'd hidden him. As I began to drag him toward the road I heard a faint voice calling, "Boy . . . oh, Boy."

I dropped the policeman and looked around. "Over here," called the voice. "I'm at the window."

The window was dirty, but through it I saw the old lady that Donna warned me about. "Come here," she called, and I walked over to the window. I stopped short so she couldn't grab me.

"Hello," I said.

"I have a favor to ask of you," she said. She was very old and brittle. Her voice was cracked and her whole body shook back and forth as if she were the most scared person in the world. "My pet bird died, and I wish you would bury it for me."

"Sure."

"Oh, thank you," she said. "I've had him for a long time and I think he deserves a proper burial." She reached forward with her shaky hand and gave me a small paper bag. "His name is Victor," she said. "He was good company."

"I'll bury him right now," I said. "In the field."

"That's fine," she said. "By the way, you can keep that policeman in my yard so the boys won't drag it off every night."

"Thanks." I looked at my watch. "I've got to get going." She nodded her head up and down as she backed away from the window and slipped deeper into the gray light of the trailer. She looked like someone drowning.

I ran out to the road. Donna wasn't in sight. I crossed into the field on the other side and began to dig a hole by kicking up the sand and stones with the back of my shoe. I knew if Donna caught me I'd never have a second chance with her. She *hated* the old lady and she'd think I was an *idiot* for helping. When I thought the hole was deep enough, I put the bag in and covered it over. Then I searched around for pieces of rocks and shells to cover the grave and to spell out the name VICTOR.

"What are you doing?" It was Donna.

I jumped up and looked at her as if she were a crazed murderer who'd escaped from a mental institution.

"You're doing something for that old lady, aren't you?"

"Yes."

"Well, you shouldn't. Once you start doing things for her she'll be after you every morning. Why'd you think I quit? Are you burying something for her?"

"Her bird died," I said. "There's nothing wrong with helping her."

"Yeah, I buried her other bird. Only, when I looked in the bag it wasn't a bird but an old chicken leg. I told you, she's nuts."

"Well, I looked in the bag," I said, lying. "It was a bird."

"I don't believe you. You're stupid if you do anything else for that old basket case."

I didn't know what to say.

"So long, sucker," she yelled back at me as she rode away. I felt like running after her and shoving her off her bike, but I didn't. I finished spelling out VICTOR, pushed the policeman into the bushes, and went to class.

On the way home Gary Rook wanted to know if I'd help him knock down a wasps' nest in his carport.

"Forget it," I said. "After your sister almost killed me I don't want to play at your house."

"Don't worry about her," he said. "She and Mom made up."

That's what worries me, I thought. They make up one day so they can try and kill each other the next. They should both be arrested for soap-opera behavior.

I rode past the drive-in and stopped at Woolworth's. They had a pet department with singing canaries and parakeets. I looked them over carefully. I didn't want to buy a dud, so I decided on the canary. It cost ten dollars, a lot of money. But Victor must have meant a lot to her.

Back in my room, I unlocked my diary. I kept all my money taped between the pages. I counted the bills and the change. I still only had eight dollars.

"Hey, son," Dad called as he passed by my bedroom. "Get ready for dinner."

When we all sat down at the table, Betsy served. She'd made spaghetti.

"We're having an audit at the bank this week," Mom said. "I'm going to be coming home a couple of hours later than usual."

"Jack, that means you're going to have to help out more around the house."

"What's that mean, Dad? I already do the yard work and garbage. It should be Betsy's job to do the housework."

"Betsy already does more than her share with cleaning and laundry and now cooking," said Mom. "You can do the dishes."

"Not the dishes," I moaned. I had almost been flattened by Gary's sister, I'd blown it with Donna Lowry, and now I had to do the dishes for my sister.

"Well, I'll make you a deal," Dad said. "You do the dishes one week and Betsy can do them the next."

"Okay. But she starts this week." I didn't want to have to do the spaghetti dishes.

"We'll flip a coin." Dad fished a quarter out of his pocket. "Loser washes for the first week."

"Okay," I agreed reluctantly.

Dad flipped the coin. "Your call," he said to Betsy.

"Heads," she yelled.

It landed in his hand and he slapped it down on his forearm. "Heads it is," he announced. "Jack does the dishes."

"Loser," Betsy said under her breath.

"People can be arrested for using children as slave labor," I mumbled, but nobody paid any attention to me.

While they finished dinner I put together a plan. I started to eat very slowly. Before long, everyone had finished eating and excused themselves, but I still had food on my plate. I drank my water slowly. I buttered another piece of bread. I helped myself to more spaghetti.

When Betsy walked by, I said, "This sure is good spaghetti."

"What a pig you are," she shot back. "Look at you. People are starving all over the world and you eat not because you need to but just because you like the taste of it."

When I finished that plate I served myself another. I looked at my watch. An hour had gone by. Mom and Betsy hadn't lifted a finger in the kitchen. I served myself a third, then a fourth plate. I will eat all night long if I have to. When they get up for breakfast, I'll still be sitting here, eating. By then, they'll clean up the kitchen just because they can't stand to see it so messy.

But after a few more bites I couldn't eat any more. I pushed myself away from the table and staggered into the living room.

"I don't feel so good," I said to Mom. "I think I'm going to throw up."

"It's no wonder you feel sick," she replied. "You just ate four plates of spaghetti."

"I hope you heave all over yourself," Betsy sneered.

"I hope I heave on you," I replied, then dashed down the hall and into the bathroom. I leaned over the toilet and threw up. It looked like bloody worms. I flushed the toilet and moaned loudly.

"Mom, I don't think I can do the dishes," I said when she checked on me.

"You know as well as I do that you made yourself sick," she said. "Now, make sure you clean up your mess, and then do the dishes. And no more of your nonsense."

As I washed the dishes I began to sing about the hills being alive with music. But instead of making me crazy, it gave me the perfect idea. I finished the dishes in record time, got dressed in my grubby clothes, and snuck out of the house. I grabbed a trash bag from the utility room and walked down to the drive-in theater. There was a hole cut in the chain-link fence and I slipped through just as the von Trapp family ran a forty-yard dash and sang without breathing hard.

There were bottles and cans just below all the car windows. I had to move quickly. I didn't want to be missed at home. I darted between the cars and picked up the cans and searched through the garbage bin until I had two dollars' worth. The bag was so full it wouldn't fit through the hole in the fence, so I had to unload half of it and then reload it on the other side. Then I ran home.

I woke late and had to ride like a maniac so I could be on time to roll the tin policeman into the middle of the road. I was out of breath but excited. I had enough money in cans and bottles to buy the canary. Still, it bothered me what Donna had said about the chicken bone, so I checked on my grave. A dog had dug it up and there were feathers and a piece of dried-up bird leg next to the ripped-open bag. I felt good knowing that Donna was wrong and I was right. But I felt bad about Victor and reburied him.

At lunchtime, Mrs. Marshall asked me to stay behind. "I'm sorry to tell you this," she said sternly, "but I'm taking back your Safety Patrol badge."

"Why?"

"Donna said you weren't doing a good job. Said you were spending your time talking to someone in a house trailer. She wants to rejoin and I'm giving the badge back to her.

She's never caused me a bit of trouble and I can see that you aren't cut out for the job."

I turned and walked out of the room. I knew I was being disrespectful, but I didn't care. I rode my bike home as hard as I could. If I see Donna in the street, I thought, I'll flatten her. I'll call her a liar and then I'll run her over.

I didn't have time to eat lunch. I grabbed my bag of cans and bottles and took them to the Piggly Wiggly supermarket and redeemed them for two dollars. Then I went next door to Woolworth's and bought the canary. It seemed very happy in its cardboard cage and chirped all the way home. I put it in my room and raced to school. I made it back just in time. Still, Mrs. Marshall gave me a dirty look as I took my seat.

After school, I went home and got the bird. Suddenly, I was nervous. I didn't know if the old lady wanted another bird. If she didn't, I'd have to talk Mom into keeping it or tell Woolworth's the bird had a disease, like beak rot, and they'd have to give me my money back. I put the cage in my bike basket and headed for Donna's corner.

She was dragging the policeman across the road.

"Thanks a lot for telling Mrs. Marshall I was doing a lousy job," I said.

"You should be mad at yourself for hanging around that old nut," she said right back.

"I can do anything I feel like doing. Any time I feel like doing it."

"You aren't going to give that old witch a bird, are you?" she asked, rolling her eyes.

"Mind your own business."

"She'll probably cook it."

"I wish she'd cook you."

"You're weird," Donna said, matter-of-factly. "You know I could arrest you."

"That badge doesn't mean a thing. It's fake. A real police-man would laugh at you." I reached out and tried to snatch it off her belt. I wanted to jump up and down on it, but she stepped back.

"Look out," she barked and dropped into a crouch. "I know karate." She struck a fighting pose and hissed like a snake.

"You don't scare me," I said. "You or your badge."

I turned away and crossed the street. I knocked on the old lady's door, and when she opened it, I gave her the bird.

"For you," I said.

She had a lovely smile, just like my grandmother. She was still trembling all over like a little poodle. "Why, you are a fine young man," she said in her shaky voice. "What's your name?"

"Jack," I said.

"Then I'll name the bird Jack," she said.

That was fine with me.

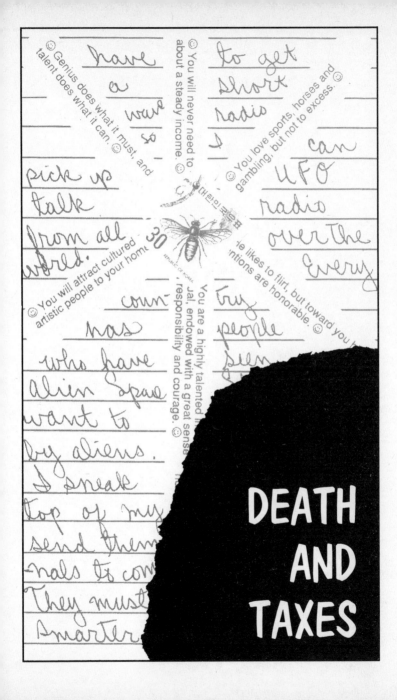

I HAD BEEN DRIVING Betsy nuts. I'm not allowed in her bedroom, but I'd been sneaking in and listening to her new radio on Saturday mornings when she takes modern-dance lessons with Sue Peabo. My radio was so old it only got the local stations. But hers got everything.

There was just one show that interested me: "The UFO Talk Line." People from all over the world called in to report UFO sightings and to explain why the government is always hiding the evidence. There were reports of a formation of silver UFOs over Brazil, and then the same ones were seen as far away as Rumania, and then back over Washington, D.C. But our government was denying any such sightings, even though a radio caller, Mr. Fralinger, had seen them with his own eyes. Each show, which was hosted by Dr. D. Beebe and sponsored by Dixie Cake Company, always had an invited guest who was either an expert or someone who had actually seen a UFO. Once they had on a lumberjack from Maine who had been captured and examined for five days by UFO doctors. After that show, I climbed up onto our house roof and sent out waves of "mental telepathy" thought messages to UFO pilots, telling them where I was and that I was willing to give up my life on earth to go live on another planet.

Dr. D. Beebe reported that the government has many crashed UFOs in warehouses and has real alien beings kept in freezers so they can study them and discover the secret of eternal life, so only the rich and powerful can live forever. "It's all a government cover-up," he insisted.

I was listening to a special report on secret UFO air bases in Peru when Betsy opened her door.

"You creep," she said. "Get out of here." Then before I could move she yelled down the hall. "Mom, he's in my room again."

Mom's voice bounced back. "Jack, leave Betsy's radio alone."

"I'm not hurting anything," I said. "I'm just listening to the radio."

"You're listening to a bunch of lunatics who take fake photographs of flying hubcaps and try and pass them off as UFOs."

"That's not all true," I replied. She was *so* wrong. "Some pictures are real. Even the government's own experts haven't proved that they're fake."

"Listen to yourself. You sound like one of the nuts who hang around the bus station selling crystals from the lost continent of Atlantis."

"You'll see someday," I said. "Just remember that there is always a Doubting Thomas."

"Don't bring religion into this," she snapped. "Or you'll be in over your head." She was right. Betsy knew all the Bible stories by heart and was constantly correcting everyone who made a mixed-up remark.

"Okay. But someday you'll see."

"I'll be long gone by then," she said. She was always saying that. She had secret plans to go to college in London.

I tuned the radio back to her station. "If my radio was any good, I wouldn't have to use yours."

"If I catch you in here again," she threatened, "I'll punch you so hard you'll see UFOs."

"Funny," I said sarcastically, "but your face beat you to it." I ran past her and was across the hall when her shoe hit me in the back of the head. Betsy couldn't throw a baseball across the yard, but she was deadly with shoes. She could throw one through a donut if I held it in front of my face.

I had to get a better radio and it had to be a shortwave radio like Dad had before it broke, so I could pick up UFO talk radio all over the world. Every country had people who had seen alien spacecrafts, and I had to know what they looked like, and if they captured people and animals, or if they thought human beings were too primitive and warlike to visit. Maybe we had diseases that would kill them, just like the American Indians died when the pioneers gave them their diseases. My theory is that humans are so inferior to aliens that they can't stand to be around us, so they turn right around and zoom back home.

Because we are always so mean to each other, they must think we would be especially mean to them. The international news reports on Dad's old shortwave radio were frightening. Countries all around the world were at war. And in America there were a lot of "little wars" that I read about in the newspaper. Wars that take place in the home. I read where most of the people murdered are murdered by friends or family members or neighbors shooting each other over parking spaces. Betsy might hit me with a shoe once a week, but it's not the same as her shooting me with a gun.

That's why it's important for me to sit on my roof at night and send thought messages to the UFOs telling them that I am a good person and that I don't like violence and I don't lie, and I want to be friends and share everything about ourselves. I wish they'd come down and take me away.

Out front, I heard Dad's pickup truck pull into the driveway. He had just changed jobs again. His old truck was yellow and it was always washed and waxed because it was Dad's job to look good as a concrete salesman. But his new truck was big and covered from top to bottom with white spray paint and muck. The back was full of paint cans, tools, and two air compressors. One was for steam-cleaning the mildew off dirty tile roofs, and the other was for spray-painting them white again. Even the inside of the cab was filthy and littered with old coffee cups, sandwich wrappers, and cigarette butts. The rig looked like it had been abandoned under a tree and was now covered with a hundred years of bird droppings. And Dad was always a mess when he came home. His pants and shirt were stiff with paint and his hair was streaked white where he had run his hands through it to keep it out of his eyes.

Mom opened the refrigerator and I heard the *pssht* sound of a beer can opening. She poured it into an ice-cold mug.

"Aren't you a sight," she said cheerfully, meeting him at the front door.

"Hey," he replied and gave her a kiss. "Meet me around back. I want to get out of these clothes."

All this week she had been really nice to him, because last week he had gone around the bend. He had received a letter from the Internal Revenue Service saying he owed the government a lot of money. After he read that letter, he cursed and stomped through the house, giving speeches to all of us. "Let me tell you the truth about our government," he said to me. "The real criminals are the politicians and bankers. Just once I'd like to see them arrest some of the thieves in Washington who pocket everything the working man makes." I wanted to tell him how the government also covers up all the UFO sightings and crashes, but I kept my mouth shut.

"You're a big mess," I heard Mom say.

"I worked like a dog today," Dad replied. "I kept thinking I was working so some congressman could send his bratty kids to college."

"Now, let's not get too worked up all over again," Mom said. "We don't know just how serious this is."

Dad showered, then got busy with sorting through our tax papers. The dining-room table was covered with stacks of shoe boxes. Each was labeled Business or Medical or Insurance or Supplies or Moving Expenses. From what Dad said, the IRS wanted to examine his business deductions for the past seven years. That's from when I started kindergarten in Pennsylvania until now, I thought. I hadn't saved anything from that time in my life, especially boxes of little receipts. It seemed unfair, as if they expected a person to save all their diapers from when they were born.

I thought it would be a good night to have everyone like me. I tried to find one thing each week that would make everyone forgive me for any of the rotten things I might have said or done during the week. "Hey, Dad," I asked quietly, "would you like your shoes polished?"

"Yeah. Sure," he said abruptly, without looking up. He was adding a stack of figures and I could faintly hear him counting to himself. I got his shoes, Mom's high heels, Betsy's school flats, Pete's good Sunday loafers, and all of mine, and went out to the screened-in porch. I polished Dad's good shoes first, then took a wire brush and scraped off all the mud and paint from his work boots. I tugged on the leather insoles until they came free, then poured a layer of baking soda on them to draw out the nasty, damp smell. There was a slight breeze and from across the canal I could hear the Diehls' television. "The Jeffersons" was coming on next. I sang along with the theme. "Movin' on up . . ." The song was like gospel music, which I liked to sing. My favorite was one called "Jesus Dropped the Charges!" I imagined going up to heaven and meeting Jesus, who was a big black man with a chorus of angels. I would list all my sins and Jesus would forgive me and then we'd all sing, "Jesus dropped the charges!" We'd dance around on the clouds, clap our hands, and sing like there was no tomorrow.

The telephone rang and Mom answered it in the kitchen. "Hello?" she said, in her professional bank-teller voice. Then suddenly her voice tightened like a rope. "Just tell me, Jim," she snapped, and in a few seconds she cried out, "Oh, my God, no."

Dad jumped up from the table. "What?" he asked. Mom was crying so hard she just passed the telephone to Dad. After listening a moment, he spoke evenly to Uncle Jim: "We'll leave tonight and see you in a day or so."

I knew someone must have died but I didn't know who. The only time I heard Mom's voice sound so intense was when Pete was dying. He hadn't learned how to walk yet and

Mom had him in the playpen. He reached between the bars and ripped a leaf off a house plant and tried to swallow it. When she found him, he was blue. That's when I heard her voice snap: "Jack, call your father at work! The number's above the phone!" By the time he arrived, Mom had flipped Pete upside down and with her long fingernails had finally gouged out the leaf.

I felt horrible as I stood on the porch with a shoe in each hand. I was going over in my mind who I would least want to die. Not my grandparents or uncles and aunt. Not their children. Not my great-uncles or even my second cousins. I didn't want anyone to die. But one of them had already been chosen.

I wiped my eyes against my shoulders. Pete was crying and hugging Mom around the waist. Betsy was blowing her nose into a tissue. Mom's face was set crookedly, and then a low moan rose up out of her like an air bubble coming from deep underwater, and then more moans that turned into the word "God." "Oh, God. Oh, God. Oh, God."

Dad hugged her from behind and held her up. "God. God. God," she cried. "Why?"

I took my place next to Betsy. "It's Grandpap," she whispered.

Dad woke me up at three in the morning. "It's time, son," he said. I jumped out of bed as if I had never slept.

"What can I do?" I asked.

"Get washed up and help your mother load the trunk."

I took my duffel bag out to the kitchen. Mom was wrapping sandwiches and hard-boiled eggs in aluminum foil. We packed up the trunk and laid out our good clothes on top of the luggage. "Is this all that's going?" I asked. She said it was, and when I closed the trunk she began to cry again.

BoBo was barking from my bedroom window when we pulled out of the driveway. "Did you close your bedroom door?" I asked Betsy.

"Of course," she said. "That brain-dead dog's going to chew up everything in the house."

We each sat next to a window in the back seat. Pete slept between us, his head on Betsy's lap and his feet on mine. Mom had called Steve Smith, a kid who lived down the street, who made a business out of taking care of people's pets while they were on vacation. He was cheaper than the kennel. Maybe Mom will let me call him and tell him to close my door. But I doubt she'd let me make a long-distance call.

After a few miles on the Florida Turnpike, I fell asleep. When I woke up it was light outside and I saw cows in the fields. "Where are we?" I asked.

"Kissimmee," answered Mom. She was the navigator and it was always her job to call out the road signs and plan our routes and handle the tolls.

"How're you doing, Dad?" I asked. Mom didn't know how to drive, and so I thought it was smart to ask him questions and keep him alert.

"I'm hanging in there." In one of his *Popular Science* magazines a man invented a hat that had a built-in alarm, so that if your head slumped over, the alarm would go off and wake you up. Dad always drove straight through from our house to Pennsylvania without stopping to sleep. He wanted to save money by not staying in a motel. But I knew he really liked it when we arrived and my uncles slapped him on the back, saying things like "I never could have done it without stopping," or "You're a better man than I." And even if we arrived around breakfast time, they always welcomed him with a cold beer.

Mom poured Dad a cup of coffee from the thermos. I started thinking of our car as if we were in a cross-country race. I imagined a big number 3 painted on our roof. Every time we passed a car I felt closer to being in first place. But I hated it when we stopped for gas and all those cars passed us by. I especially hated how long it took everyone to use the bathroom. Dad was in and out like a veteran race driver. I followed his example. Mom and Betsy were slow, and Pete was a snail. When we stopped in Georgia, Mom sent me in after him.

"What are you doing?" I asked. He had fallen asleep while sitting on the toilet with his chin in his hands. "Hey! We're losing the race!" I yelled, clapping my hands. He sat up and tripped forward over his pants. His head hit me in the stomach and knocked the wind out of me. I fell over into a puddle of unknown liquid. "Just my luck," I muttered. "This stuff will rot my pants."

"What's the next town?" Dad asked when we were back on the highway.

"The sign says 'Trash Barrel' ahead," Mom replied and began to search the map. "I can't find Trash Barrel anywhere on this map," she said. Betsy looked over at me. I wasn't going to say anything. Then we saw Dad grinning at us in the mirror and making the "crazy" sign with his finger twirling around his ear.

"Oh, God," Mom said and burst out laughing. "I am losing my mind." She laughed at herself and we all joined her and had an even bigger laugh when we passed "Trash Barrel."

We drove on through Georgia, South Carolina, and

North Carolina. When we reached Virginia, Mom wanted to change places with me so she could stretch out. I had been waiting for the opportunity to get at the radio. Once she got settled, I began searching the AM band for a UFO talk line. "Hey, Dad, do you believe in UFOs?" I asked.

"Just death and taxes," he said dryly. "I only believe in what I can see and feel. There are no such things as UFOs."

"How do you know?"

"I know. Besides, there is no proof."

"But a million people have seen them."

"And people used to think the world was flat," he replied. "If I see it, I'll believe it."

"What about things you can't see?" I asked. "What about things like luck and God?"

"If I can't see it, I don't believe it," he said.

On the few Sundays we went to church, he stayed out in the car and read the newspaper. Once I overheard him say to Mom that only hypocrites went to church and that the good people stayed at home and lived decent lives. "That's just an excuse to be lazy," she had replied. "Besides, you're going to confuse the children."

He had me confused. If he didn't believe in God, maybe he believed in luck. "Hey, Dad, was it just bad luck that you got caught cheating on your taxes?"

He flared up. "I didn't cheat on my taxes. I'm being robbed by the government so another congressman can take a Hawaiian vacation. But you," he said, pointing at me, "can go to the loony bin for believing in UFOs. Take a good look at your uncle Will. He's a real flake and he claims to have seen UFOs."

"Really?"

"That's what he claims," Dad said. "But everyone knows that Will doesn't know his ass from his elbow."

It was lucky Mom was asleep. I knew better than to get him talking like that. I couldn't wait to see Uncle Will. I always thought he was a bit strange, but now I realized that he was just misunderstood, like a lot of people who had seen UFOs. "Do you think it's bad luck that Grandpap had a heart attack?" I asked, changing the subject.

"It isn't good or bad luck. It's just part of life. I had a friend who was hit by lightning on the golf course. He had three young kids. And look at Johnny Foil. Nobody knows when their time will come. Grandpap probably died from working so hard in the coal mines all his life."

When I was little, I used to sit on his basement stairs and wait for him to come home from the mines. He was black with coal dust, and he had his own shower down there. He would put his miner's helmet on my small head and turn on the light and I'd play like I was digging coal. Then he'd open his lunch bucket and give me a piece of pickle he had saved just for me. I'd suck the vinegar out of it while he showered, and then he'd sit me down on his thigh and give me a horse ride while he sang, "Rattle up a june bug . . . A penny royal tea . . . Cat's in the cupboard and can't see me."

I tried to keep Dad awake by talking, and even though I was excited to question Uncle Will, I still fell asleep.

When I woke, there was snow on the ground and my face was cold from pressing against the window. Mom leaned forward from the back seat and began to straighten up my hair. I knew we must be close. She picked at the sleep in the corner of my eyes, then licked her thumb and wiped a smudge off my chin. Betsy started to brush out her long hair, and then Pete woke, so Mom started to work on him.

We pulled into the driveway and up to the garage. Uncle Will and Uncle Jim came around the back of the house to greet us. Mom began to cry. Uncle Jim was holding a beer in one hand and wiping tears away with the other. "How you doing," he managed to say to Dad as he got out of the car.

"I don't know," Dad said roughly. "If the good Lord don't get you, then the tax man will."

"Hush," Mom snapped.

"I'm sorry," Dad said. He seemed to be speaking to all of us. "Lately, it all seems like death and taxes. A man just can't get ahead these days."

Uncle Will kicked at the ground. Dad looked away. Aunt Nancy peeked around the corner of the house, her eyes as pink as a rabbit's.

Grandma was in her bedroom, and after Mom saw her, she said it would be best to let her rest and just see the adults for now.

I was disappointed. I had been thinking of so many things to say to her. How sorry I was and how much I loved her. I drifted around the house, trying to find something to do, and soon I was thinking about Uncle Will. After what Dad had said I looked at him differently. His head was rounder than everyone else's in the family. Maybe UFO doctors had worked on him. He had a lot of strange scars, but I knew they were from getting dragged down a hill by a car when he was my age. He had metal pins in his legs and a metal plate in his head. I had always wanted to hold a giant magnet up to him and see if he would slide across the room and stick to it. He was the youngest in Mom's family, and she and Uncle Jim still teased him, like Betsy and I teased Pete. Before I asked him about the UFOs, I knew I'd have to wait for the right time when we were alone.

Betsy and I were playing pick-up-sticks in the kitchen when Uncle Jim said to me, "I'll drive you out to Jackson's house. You can stay there with Dale." Dale was my second cousin. Whenever we visited, all of us kids got paired up with other cousins our own age. I liked staying with him because they didn't have indoor plumbing, so at night, instead of going outside to the outhouse in the dark and cold, we just opened a window and peed down into the flower beds.

Aunt Stella had my favorite dinner waiting for me when I arrived. First, we all got a big hunk of fresh baloney that she cut off a huge pink coil that looked like a giant pig's tail. And then we all got our own big mixing bowl full of her homemade berry ice cream. For dessert, we had oatmeal cookies the size of dinner plates. She was the smartest cook because she made what we really wanted to eat, not what some school nurse said we had to eat.

They didn't have a television so Dale and I went to bed early. But in the middle of the night I woke up with a stomachache and had to go to the outhouse. I was already half dressed because it was cold in the house. I put on my shoes and Dale's heavy coat and made my way downstairs and out the back door. They lived far out in the country, away from city lights, so the sky was clear and filled with a million stars. I looked up and saw the Milky Way, the Big Dipper, and Mars. I spotted a few green-and-red satellites, but no UFOs. It was too cold to stand still, and by the time I reached the outhouse, I was frozen stiff. With my luck, I thought, my butt will stick to the seat and I'll freeze to death.

When I finished, I stepped out and heard someone talking. There was a light coming from a split in the barn doors, and I crept up to take a look. Inside, three women were walking in a circle while praying. "Please heal these chickens," one called out.

"Amen," said another.

I turned and ran back to the house. "Hey, Dale," I said when I got upstairs. "There are women in your barn praying for the chickens."

"Oh, yeah," he said sleepily. "Mom let some Christian Scientist ladies pray over 'em. There's no cure for what they got, so she figured to give these ladies a chance."

"Does this seem weird to you?" I asked.

"Sure does," he said. "But if it works, I won't knock it."

"I guess so." I crawled into bed.

In the morning, I went back outside to pump some water up from the well. Stella said she would heat it up for me so I could wash properly before the funeral. Jackson came out of the barn with a wheelbarrow stacked high with frozen chickens.

"They can pray all they want," he said as he passed by. "I believe in prayer, mind you, but ain't no prayers gonna save these chickens."

After a breakfast of ice cream and hot chocolate, Uncle Jim arrived. He told Jackson there was trouble with digging the grave. "The ground is so frozen they have to set fires and then can only dig down half a foot at a time," he said.

"They could keep him in the icebox at the morgue until the spring thaw," Jackson suggested.

"I already mentioned it to Mom," he said, meaning

Grandma. "But she won't hear of it. Says she won't rest and he won't rest till his body's properly buried."

"Can't say as I blame her," Jackson said. "I'll take a run over there and see. They might need some extra wood. Hey, Dale and Jake," he hollered from the porch, using my nickname, "go fill the truck up with firewood."

After we piled the wood up over the dead chickens, Dale and I jumped into the cab. Even with gloves and two pairs of socks, my hands and feet were freezing. Dale started the engine and turned on the heater. Jackson hopped in and we took off for the cemetery.

"Jim said you can ride to the funeral with us," he said as we drove through Mount Pleasant. We passed the hospital where I was born. We had moved out of town seven years before and I didn't recognize anything else. The old cemetery was on a steep hill. A highway crew was salting and sanding the ice on the road.

"These are some of your 'pap's friends," Jackson pointed out as he waved to them. "They wouldn't come out here for just anyone."

Up at the grave site two workmen were in a hole about three feet deep. We unloaded the wood and they set it up for a fire in the grave. They poured gasoline over the logs and threw a match to it. It caught with a *whoosh*.

"Don't worry," said one of the men who was wearing a football helmet to keep his head warm. "We'll be ready for you at two."

"Hey, Dale," I whispered, "does all this seem weird to you, or is it just new to me?"

"It must just be new to you," Dale said. "Seems about the same to me."

•

We came back at two. The cemetery crew was just unrolling fake grass around the grave and driving in the last of the iron tent stakes. Mom and Grandma were in the back seat of Dad's car. No one else was with them, so I opened the front door and slipped in. It was warm inside. Dad had the radio news on. "How's it going?" I asked. I still didn't know what to say to Grandma.

"I don't know why I listen to this damn radio," he said under his breath. "They catch one congressman having hanky-panky with his secretary and they catch another taking kickbacks from a rocket manufacturer and so they slap their hands and send them both to a luxury prison in Arizona. Now, how much do you think that cost the taxpayer?"

I was silent. Maybe it was a trick question and there was no answer.

"Jack," Mom said, "would you like to say something to your grandmother? She's been wanting to know where you've been hiding."

I wasn't sure if Mom was rescuing me from Dad or scolding me.

Grandma smiled at me. She was wearing all black, with a veil over her pale face. "Hi, pumpkin," she said and held my hand.

"I'm really sorry," I said. "I love Grandpa and said my prayers for him." That was all I could say before my throat tightened up. She squeezed my hand and I squeezed hers back. I turned my head away but kept holding on.

"It's always the good ones that go before their time," Dad said out loud. "The lousy ones are left alive—"

"That's not necessary for you to say," Mom cut in.

"Bye, Grandma," I said quickly and stepped out of the car. By then, the tent was ready and the bright green plastic grass was in place. Soon Dad and my uncles and Grandpap's younger brothers carried the coffin to the rope sling that would lower it down into the ground. But first they opened the coffin for one last look. He still seemed like Grandpap, only he was pink with makeup, like an old black-and-white photograph that was hand-painted. Mom lined us up and one by one we went up to him. I took a little school picture of myself out of my wallet, and when it was my turn I tried to slip it into his jacket pocket. But the pocket was sewn shut. I dropped it down into the satin lining, then pulled my hand away as I said a prayer and goodbye.

It was so cold I couldn't cry much. But when Grandma fell across his body, crying, "Jim, Jim, don't leave me," I burst into tears. Mom and Uncle Will gently pulled her off, and Mr. Gotts, the funeral director, closed the casket and sealed it. They lowered it into the hole. The preacher gave a short blessing, and we all filed back to the cars, with Grandma crying out between breaths.

The after-the-funeral party was held at Grandma's house. People from all over came to say how sorry they were. They brought trays of food, which overlapped each other across the long kitchen table. Since Grandma stayed in her bedroom, they mostly left after a cup of coffee.

It was dark when I found Uncle Will sitting alone in the living room. He looked tired, but I had to talk to him, because we were returning to Florida in the morning. "Uncle Will," I said quietly, "I heard you saw a UFO. I believe in UFOs, too. What did it look like?"

"I didn't see it up close," he said, "but it came in real slow,

down from Canada. It looked like a meteor with a fire tail,
but the folks who saw it in the air say it steered around like
it was looking for a place to land. Then it went down in the
woods behind the Yablonskys' farm. A bunch of us were
parked up on the ridge and saw like a whitish-blue light
glowing, then fading back up in the trees. We didn't get
down to it, but the fire company had gone out there because
of the possibility of it being a small plane or something. The
army hadn't arrived yet to chase everyone out, so some folks
came up to it in the woods and saw it real good."

"Wow." I sighed. "Was it broken open? Were there
aliens?"

"Tell you what. I've had about all this party I can handle.
Let's take a ride over to the fire station and you can talk to
the guy who touched it."

I started to put my coat on when Mom saw me. "What are
you up to?" she asked.

"Will's gonna take me to where he saw the UFO." I could
tell she wasn't in the mood to hear about spaceships after she
had been sitting with Grandma for two days.

Will came around the corner. "I'm gonna take him with
me for a few minutes. I'll bring him back in one piece. Don't
worry, if he's a pest I'll ship him off to Mars."

"Okay," Mom said and rolled her eyes at me. "Just make
certain you have your stuff packed and ready for tomorrow."

We jumped in Will's huge Oldsmobile and sped off down
a dark road until we came to the town of Hecla and pulled
up to the fire station. "Hey, Jerry," Will called out as he
lifted the garage door. "My nephew wants to hear your
spaceship story."

Jerry was short and sturdy. He had a fluffy head of white
hair as thick and woolly as sheep. "Sorry to hear about your

dad," he said to Will. He set his cup of coffee next to the radio scanner, then turned to me. He didn't miss a beat.

"We came up to it from a cropping of rock and it was down in a gully. It had not started glowing blue just yet. You could feel the heat coming off it, but there was no fire and it was in one piece, about the shape of a doorknob and about the size of a car. I could see a path of trees it had bowled down, but it wasn't scratched. The hardest metal I've ever seen, looked like a blue copper. I rapped on it with my flashlight and it was like hitting solid rock. No echo and no vibration. I had hollered out that I found it and a couple of the volunteers came and saw it. The strangest part was the writing all over it, like it had been drawn on with a welding torch. I ain't seen no writing like it, and since then I studied up on every form of writing known to man, past and present. It was totally foreign. I only wish I had a camera. And then the state police come up and run us off. Said the army didn't want anyone messing with it. As soon as I turned to go, that's when it started to glow blue, and I ran for my life, thought the thing might blow up."

"That's amazing," I said. I wanted to remember every word he spoke. I had to write *this* down when we returned to Florida.

"Yeah. And when I got back here to the station, the army had arrived and taken over our phones, and I was told by a four-star general to keep my mouth shut if I knew what was good for me. Top Secret, he warned me."

"From where I was," said Will, "it started glowing when the army arrived. Then they brought in a huge truck like a tank carrier and a crane and they loaded it up, put a tarp over it, and drove on out of there."

"I called the newspapers and the state cops and the local

army reserve and all of them said they hadn't heard a thing about it," Jerry added. "I called my congressman and he reported back that there never was no sighting. If that isn't a government cover-up, then I don't know what is."

"Wow," I said. "Can I shake your hand?"

He stuck out his thick hand and I shook the hand that touched a UFO. "You gotta believe that they're out there," he insisted. "I'll go to my grave knowing the truth of what I seen, and no army or government or some of these Bible-thumping folks around here are gonna make me think different."

When we got back in the car, Uncle Will told me that most people think Jerry's gone insane. "People are nice to him to his face, but down at the fireman's club he's always talked about as a 'space shot.' "

"Do you mean that I shouldn't believe him?" I asked.

"Believe what you want to believe," he replied, confusing me even more.

On the dark ride back to Jackson's, I began to think about returning home. What a wreck, I thought. Dad is going to have to face the Internal Revenue Service, which will make him angry every day. BoBo has probably torn my bedroom to shreds, and Mom will be heartbroken. I'll be behind in school and have a pile of homework waiting for me. I wished a UFO would come down and capture me. Just lift me off the ground and take me far away. Maybe that's why I believe in them, I thought; they'll take me away from all this confusion and set me down in a place without fear.

Frankie Pagoda. He was standing on the top of his roof in his bathing suit. From my front yard I waved to him. He waved back. "Hey, watch this!" he yelled. He crouched down then shot forward down the back side of his roof. I knew what he was up to. He was going to jump into his swimming pool. But just then I heard a loud thud a scream. I ran yard and arou I couldn't bel the pool by and hit so then flatte the concre was bloo he got to

MY BROTHER'S ARM

D AD COULDN'T STAND the Pagoda family, our right-side next-door neighbors. He said they had all lost control of their senses. "Just look at 'em," he hollered when he watched them do something weird like paint a giant atomic-bomb target on their roof. "They are out of control. The parents just let those kids get away with anything." The oldest, Gary, had just been sent to a juvenile prison for stealing cars. Frankie was my age. His whole face was still bruised from when he dove off the roof into their swimming pool. He was a little short with his leap and hit his forehead on the concrete edge around the pool. The whites of his eyes were still blood-red. And Suzie, his twin sister, had just tried to dye her brown hair blond with Clorox, but it turned from brown to green. Mr. and Mrs. Pagoda bred show dog poodles for a living. *Inside* their house they must have had thirty dogs in cages. Every time I visited them, I took a deep breath of fresh air before I stepped inside. It was the last chance for good air, because the house smelled nasty, like dog crap and piss and damp fur. It made me gag and my eyes sting. And when I left their house my clothes smelled like a used diaper.

Frankie and I were building a tree fort around the far side of their house. We were finishing one started by his older brother before he was arrested. The platform was in place and we were adding new ladder rungs to climb up the outside of the trunk.

"Let's build a roof," I suggested to Frankie. "Then when it rains we can stay in the tree."

"What about lightning?" he asked.

I thought that was a dumb question coming from someone who's roof-dived into swimming pools. He also had a spiraling scar up and over his shoulder from being hit by a boat propeller while water-skiing on old snow skis. "We'll put a lightning rod on top of the tree," I said, "and run a wire down to a bucket, and if lightning strikes, one of us can put it over his head and be turned into Frankenstein's monster."

Frankie laughed. He always laughed at my dumb ideas— which encouraged me to say and do dumb things.

"Yeah. We can do anything we want. It's our tree fort."

Pete had been snooping around our yard looking for me and now I watched him run over to the tree.

"What are you guys doing?" he asked, panting.

"What's it look like?" I said.

"We're building a clubhouse," Frankie explained.

"But you can't join," I said. "It's private."

"I'll tell Mom," he said, meaning that he'll tell that I'm in the Pagodas' yard. Dad had told us not to play here. "If old man Pagoda had a brain, he'd be dangerous," Dad said, and, "If brains were dynamite, she couldn't blow her nose."

I groaned. "All right. You can join. But you have to pass the initiation. You have to play Barnum and Bailey Circus Dare."

"Okay," he agreed, without asking what it was.

I pulled a long plank from the woodpile and set it under the tree. Then I put a round piece of log under the middle of the plank, like a seesaw. "You stand on the low end of the plank, facing out," I instructed. He did, as I climbed up into the tree fort. "When I jump on the high end," I shouted, "you fly up in the air and do a front flip."

"Okay," he said.

I jumped and landed with both feet on top of the board. Pete flew straight up in the air, just like in the circus. He flipped forward and landed on his butt. He laughed and hopped right up. "Let's do it again," he shouted.

"This time, go straight up and try to land on Frankie's shoulders," I said and placed Frankie in the right spot. When I jumped, he flew up, and on the way down he stepped on Frankie's bruised face instead of his shoulders.

Frankie dropped to the ground and howled. "He's re-broken my nose," he cried.

"Come here," I ordered and looked him over. "Naw, you're fine."

"One more time," begged Pete.

"Okay, do a back flip." I climbed the tree and jumped. When I landed on the board, Pete shot straight up. Then he threw his head back and flipped around wildly like a dropped cat. He landed with a thud on his back, then jumped right up.

"Wow," he said. "I'm dizzy."

Then I saw his arm. His forearm had hit the edge of the plank and now he had a second elbow between his old elbow and his wrist. I thought I was going to be sick.

"Can we do it again?" he asked, as his broken arm flopped over to one side.

Frankie turned his head away and started to gag. Pete gave me a funny look. Maybe I can just walk away, I thought, and in an hour he'll finally discover the break and wonder how it happened. But I couldn't. I just pointed at his arm and made a scared, moaning noise.

Then he saw it. "Aghhh!" he wailed and looked up at my face as if I had stabbed him.

"I didn't mean it," I cried. "Honest."

He turned and ran. I was right behind him. "Don't tell on me," I begged. "Please don't tell."

He screamed and his helpless arm flopped left and right with his running.

"You can have my stamp collection," I said.

He hollered even louder. "Mommmmm!"

"You can have my marble collection," I said.

He yelled in great long shrieks.

We had reached the front door of our house. "You can have my allowance for life," I said. "For *life*," I repeated.

"Daaaaaad!" he screeched.

I blocked the doorway. "Just remember, when you thought you shot down the airplane I was really nice to you."

"Mommmmm!"

I opened the door for him. I didn't know yet if he turned me down or if he just wasn't listening.

Mom dashed out of the hallway like a sprinter. "Oh, what

happened!" she asked and then saw that his arm was broken before I said it. Pete held it up for her to examine as he gasped for breath. Tears ran down through the dirt on his face.

"It looks bad," she said firmly, "but we can fix it." She turned to me and I flinched. "Jack," she ordered, "go get your father. He's in the shower."

I wanted to turn and run. I knew Dad's first question was going to be, "How'd it happen?" I opened the bathroom door and hollered in, "Hey, Dad, Mom needs you." I didn't say what was wrong, because I knew that most accidents happen in the shower and I didn't want to shout out, "Pete shattered his arm!" and have Dad get worked up and slip in the shower and break something of his. I imagined Mom having to drive us all to the hospital, and since she can't drive, we'd get into a flaming accident and in one day I could be responsible for wiping out our entire family.

"What's she want?" Dad asked, sputtering under the shower nozzle.

"Well, Pete busted his arm, and when you get a chance, they need a ride to the hospital," I explained, trying to stay calm during an emergency like in safety films at school.

"Jesus," he cursed. "As soon as I turn my back on you kids, something happens." He turned up the water pressure and slapped water at himself. "I'll be right out," he gurgled.

When they returned from the hospital, I was in my room. What Dad had said got me thinking. "It's true that as soon as you turn your back, or as soon as you think nothing bad can happen, it does," I'd written in my diary. "Just look at the *Titanic*. The captain said, 'Even God can't sink this ship.'

Then, on the first voyage across the Atlantic Ocean, *boom,* it hit an iceberg and sank. And as soon as a daredevil utters the words 'piece of cake' before attempting a stunt, he is doomed. 'Piece of cake' becomes his 'famous last words.' Mom says she can wait all day for a delivery truck to arrive, then as soon as she runs the bathtub and gets in, the doorbell rings. And when I was little, Dad bought a convertible. Every time we took a drive with the top down, it rained."

I reread everything I had written, then locked up the diary again and hid it under my mattress.

On the way from the hospital, Mom and Dad had stopped at the grocery store and let Pete pick out dinner. When they arrived home Dad started the grill on the back patio. I set the picnic table. Mom made potato salad and Betsy picked limes off the tree in the back yard for limeade.

"Anything else I can get you?" I asked Pete as I passed by him. He was sucking milk through a strawberry-flavored straw.

"Your marble collection," he said quietly.

"No way," I muttered. He was becoming more like Betsy every day. "You told on me."

"I didn't tell *how* you did it."

He hadn't. He told Dad he "fell" across the board.

After dinner I went into my bedroom and began to sort through my marbles. I picked out most of the ones I didn't want, and threw in a few beauties to trick Pete into thinking I was giving him my whole collection. Dad would go nuts if he knew how I broke Pete's arm. He'd probably take *me* out to the back yard and start flipping me up into the air like a moon shot until I crashed and burned.

I was sitting on my rug when Dad drifted into the room

and sat on the corner of my bed. This is it, I thought, I'm dead.

"I just want to talk with you for a moment," he said. I took a deep breath.

"It's your responsibility to take care of your younger brother." He stated this as a fact.

"I know," I replied, "but bad things happen when you least expect them."

"Yeah, only it's called not paying attention to what you're doing."

"I'm sorry," I said. If I could apologize fast enough, he might go away.

"Just keep it in mind," he continued, "that paying attention to what you are doing is one of the big rules in life. The sooner you learn it, the better." He winked at me, which meant the end of the conversation. Then he stood up and left the room.

A wink was not a bad ending to being "talked to." Last year, he told me about a science teacher he had in school when he was my age. The teacher had a nasty way of ending his talks. He'd built a very high and deep chair for the bad students—high and deep enough so that their shoes couldn't touch the floor. Across from them, he sat in a tall wicker chair. On the student's chair he had taped strips of metal across the seat cushion. The metal was attached to wires that ran under the chair and across the floor to an old Lionel train transformer that was beside the teacher's seat. If the student needed a rough "talking to," then at the end of the talk the teacher said, "Now let this be a lesson to you," and blasted the student from his seat with a jolt of electricity.

•

The next morning Pete knocked on my door. "I need five dollars," he said.

"I don't have five bucks."

"I'll tell Dad."

"You've become a monster," I yelled. Betsy was definitely giving him directions. "I'll work on it," I said and slammed the door.

I decided to train BoBo to be my younger brother. He was safer and cheaper. "Come on, BoBo," I sang, and the dog jumped off the bed where he was sleeping. I tied a bandanna around his neck and put a broken wristwatch on his front leg. He followed right behind me all around my room. If I could shave his body and teach him how to walk on two legs, he'd be perfect. Already, he was less trouble than Pete.

But it didn't matter. That evening, after Dad left my room for the second time in two days, I opened my diary. "Disaster," I wrote. I had just finished teaching BoBo how to tell time and was looking out the window. A few blocks away, I saw a thick cloud of smoke slowly traveling down a distant street. The houses blocked my view of where it came from. I thought it was a burning car that was still being driven. Or some strange weather condition, like a baby tornado. Then Frankie Pagoda rode his bike up our driveway. "Hurry up," he yelled through my window. "It's the mosquito fogger."

I ran outside. Pete was playing with his Lego blocks in the carport. "Where are you going?" he asked and jumped to his feet.

"To chase the fog truck," I said. "But you can't come. It's too dangerous. Dad said I have to look out for you. I won't be able to see you in all that mosquito fog even if you're an inch away from my nose, so stay put."

"You owe me five bucks," he screeched.

"I'll give it to you later," I yelled and hopped on the back of Frankie's bike. "Come on, Frankie." I slapped him like a horse. "Hurry before he catches us."

Following the fog truck was the best fun. Kids from all over rode their bikes in the cloud of dense smoke, which smelled like kerosene and billowed out of a big pipe on the back of the truck. When I was in the middle of the cloud, I couldn't see a thing. It made me feel like I was flying through the air. It was a wonderful feeling as long as you didn't collide with another kid.

Frankie and I entered the cloud from behind. I could hear the kids screaming and yelling and bikes clashing as we worked our way into it. The best part of the cloud is the solid white middle. That's the place that makes me feel like I'm drifting up over the world, empty and weightless like a hot-air balloon. The white is so dense it's like being buried in pure sugar, except it has no weight. Sometimes I can't tell up from down and I lose my balance.

Suddenly, the fogger engine stopped and the cloud lifted. There were about twenty other kids on their bikes. "Boooo! Hissss!" we shouted, like when the film breaks during a movie. "More! More!"

The driver of the truck stepped out of the cab and hopped up onto the bed of the truck. Ignoring us, he refilled the fogging engine tank with gasoline and started it up. I looked over my shoulder and spotted Pete and BoBo in the back of the pack. Pete was riding slowly because he could only use his one good arm.

"Hurry up," I hollered to him. Slowly, that huge white cloud began to cover us as we moved forward. "Where are you?" I shouted as Frankie picked up speed.

"Here," Pete said, just to my right.

"Get closer," I yelled. Then I heard the crash.

"Owwww," he cried out. "Jack!"

I hopped off the back of Frankie's bike, and when the fog
drifted away, I found him. He had collided head-on with a
mailbox on the edge of the street. He was lying in the grass
with his good hand over his mouth. BoBo was whimpering
and licking his face. "Let me see, let me see," I shouted. He
lifted his hand. His left front tooth was chipped in half. "You
might as well have my allowance for life," I said, sighing. "I
won't need it where I'm going."

After dinner, Dad had come into my room and sat on the
corner of my bed.

"What happened?" he asked.

I explained how I tried to keep Pete from following me.

"Did you ever think that you could have just turned
around and led him home?"

"No," I said.

"Don't you think you should set a good example for
him?"

"Yes," I said, feeling doomed.

"Then why don't you use your head, before you break it
open like that Pagoda kid."

"Yes," I said again.

"Or before Pete breaks his head instead of his arm or
tooth."

"Yes, Dad."

"I can't be here to watch over you kids all the time. When
I turn my back, I count on *you* to use common sense."

"Yes, Dad."

"I don't want people talking about our family the way
they talk about the Pagodas." He got up and strolled out of
the room.

Late that night, Pete began to complain that his arm hurt. If it's broken, it could be the end of my life, I thought.

"Are you sure it hurts?" Dad asked him.

Pete started to cry. They got dressed and took him to the emergency room at the hospital.

"What happened?" I asked when they returned.

"The doctor didn't set it right the first time," Mom explained. "They had to cut the cast off and reset the arm."

"How'd they do that?"

"The doctor just held it against the edge of his desk and gave it a crack."

I felt sick. "Really?"

"I know how you feel," said Mom as she ran her hand through my hair. "It was the most painful thing I ever watched."

"What did Pete do?"

"They gave him a shot of painkiller and Dad just put his hand over Pete's eyes. That was all."

"Was it because he ran into the mailbox?" I whispered, knowing how Dad thinks.

"No. This was set wrong from the beginning. So don't worry. Now go to bed, and don't say anything to your father in the morning. He's ready to sue every doctor in town."

All week long I minded my own business. When Pete asked if I wanted to sign his new cast, I refused. I didn't want to get near him. I spent my time trying to train BoBo to be a human. I slipped a T-shirt over his head and put his paws through the armholes. And I changed his name to Eric. I thought I might ride down to the Salvation Army store and buy some used baby shoes and put them on his paws.

But I was bored. I knew I shouldn't, but a few days later

I drifted over to the Pagodas'. There just wasn't anything else to do. Before I left our house, I poured Dad's Old Spice aftershave over my left hand.

"Come in," hollered Mr. Pagoda, after I knocked. I took a deep breath of air and opened the door. The smell was like sticking your head in a toilet. I held my perfumed hand to my face just about each time I took a breath. Mr. Pagoda was stirring a big pot of thick yellow goop on the stove. It boiled up and spit out of the pot like a volcano. He jumped back and shielded his eyes.

"What're you making?" I asked.

"Experimenting with banana skins," he grunted as he stirred the pot. "Everyone throws them away. If I can make something useful out of them, I'll make a fortune. Right now, I'm making a banana-skin shoe-repair kit in a can. When you get a hole in the bottom of your shoe, you just spray this stuff on and keep walking. What d'you think?"

Just then, the pot erupted and a wad of banana shoe glue hit the ceiling. It looked like it was stuck up there for life.

"Where's Frankie?" I asked, looking around.

"Out back, I think."

I nearly ran for the back door. "Air, I need air," I gasped.

Frankie was hanging conch shells on the clothesline. Conchs are hard to pull out of their shells, so he was reaching into the shell with a pair of pliers, grabbing the long, skinny foot of the conch and pinning that part over the clothesline. "This way," Frankie explained, "the heavy shell will make the conch really tired, and soon the shell will drop to the ground."

"But they're already dead," I said. "They stink."

The Pagodas were like a picture-book family I once read

about called the Stupids. Everyone knows that if you want to remove a conch from its shell you just drop it in boiling water and it comes right out.

"Why don't you do it that way?" I asked Frankie.

"Dad says it boils the color out of the shells, and he wants to sell them to tourists."

"I thought you were going to eat the conch."

"No way. They're like chewing on dog toys."

He finished pinning up the last one. "What do you want to do?" I asked.

"I have a great idea," he said. "I've been thinking about it all morning."

We went around to the swing set on the far side of his house, where my mom couldn't see us. He held up an old Hula Hoop that he had wrapped in gauze bandages. "It's a daredevil game I saw on TV. I'll get on my skateboard and ride it down the slide. You squirt lighter fluid on the gauze and set it on fire and I'll fly through it. Suzie has a Polaroid camera and she'll take pictures and we can send them in to the TV program and see if we can get on the show."

"How do I hold the burning Hula Hoop?"

"With this." He tossed me an oven mitt.

"Are you sure this will work?"

"Don't know until you try it, my dad always says."

I knew what my dad would say.

"Wait here," Frankie said. "I'll go get Suzie."

It would be neat, I thought, to see a picture of myself flying through a burning hoop on a skateboard. I'll show it to the kids at school. No one could top it.

Just then, Pete spotted me and ran over. "What're you doing?" he asked.

"Nothing that concerns you," I said sharply.

"Allowance for life," he whined. "You said so."

"It might be a short life."

Frankie and Suzie joined us.

"Okay," announced Frankie, "I'll go first."

I could see this leading to trouble. Pete will want to try it and he'll go up in flames and Dad will build a real electric chair just for me. "We have to go," I said to Frankie. "Come on, Pete." I grabbed his good arm and jerked him away.

That evening, when we sat down at the dinner table, I felt proud of myself for keeping Pete alive. I knew I couldn't tell Dad how I had used good judgment, because he would go berserk when I told him Frankie planned to skateboard through a flaming Hula Hoop. Mom dished out the corned beef and cabbage and Betsy passed out spoons.

"What's that foul smell?" Dad asked, wrinkling up his face. "What's rotting?"

"Calm down, it's just boiled cabbage," Mom said.

"I can't *calm down* with that smell coming in the windows. What is that stench?" He held his napkin up over his nose.

I knew what it was but refused to say.

"It's the conch meat," Pete shouted and pointed.

From our windows, we could see the fly-covered bodies of the conchs that Frankie had left pinned to the line after the shells had slipped off.

"God, these people are disgusting," Dad griped. "I can't wait until we move out of this neighborhood full of loonies."

"Me too," Betsy added. "Did you hear that Gary Pagoda stole another car and was caught in Miami?"

"The kid is a criminal," Dad replied. "Ugh! How do they expect us to eat dinner with that stench in the air?"

It wasn't a question anyone wanted to answer.

"Jack," he said to me, "go over there and tell those people to take down that garbage."

"Me?" I asked. "Me?"

"You," he said right back. "You know them. They're *your* friends. Now go tell them that they're smelling up the neighborhood."

I scooted back in my chair. "Okay," I said. I looked at Mom. She was no help. Betsy gave me her thin-lipped smile. Pete crossed his eyes at me. I knew what he was thinking.

I took a garbage bag from the utility room and went directly to the Pagodas' back yard. The conchs looked like diseased chicken wings. One by one, I yanked them off the line as the flies and smell swirled around my head. I didn't have gloves and the spongy meat squished between my fingers. Conch juice ran down my arm and dripped off my elbow. When I finished, I scrubbed my hands with Dad's Lava soap to get rid of the smell.

"Good job," Dad said when I returned to the table.

"Go change your shirt," Mom said. "It picked up the odor."

After dinner, Frankie knocked on my window. "Hey," he said, "my brother's back home. Do you want to watch him tattoo a naked lady on his arm?"

"I can't," I said.

After Frankie ran off I couldn't sit still. "I think it's time to go fishing, Eric," I said to BoBo. There was still plenty of light.

He looked up at me and I read his mind. Yes, Jack, I would like to go fishing, he was thinking. I unlocked my door and quietly walked down the hall with my rod in one hand and the tackle box in the other. I didn't want Pete tagging along so he could drown and ruin my life.

We went directly to a secret place behind Big Daddy's Liquors. A large water-drainage pipe emptied into a canal. I sat on the rounded edge of the pipe and opened my tackle box. I took out my net and waded into the shallow water. A small rapids formed where the water broke over the sharp rocks that narrowed the canal as it passed under an old railroad bridge. I held my net in the running water and in a few minutes I had a small shiner. "Piece of cake," I said.

I gently slipped the hook into his mouth and out his gill. I dropped him in the water and slowly let out the line. The current carried the shiner about ten yards downstream. A perfect location for a hungry snook.

After fifteen minutes, nothing happened. I figured my shiner was worn out. There was a 7-Eleven store next to the liquor store and I had enough change for a small grape Slurpee.

"Stay, Eric," I ordered BoBo and set my rod down on the pipe. "And guard that with your life." He looked up at me, then went back to sleep.

Those were my last words to him. I had taken about ten steps when I heard him yelp. When our very first BoBo was hit by a car in front of our last house, he had yelped in exactly the same way. I spun around in time to see a large alligator clamp BoBo's head in its mouth, then drag him back down the bank. BoBo's legs kicked out at the ground, but the alligator held him tight as it slithered backward down the bank and into the water.

I was terrified of the alligator. It was at least ten feet long, and I knew they were fast. Sneaky fast. I stood still for a minute. I wasn't sure what to do.

I ran back to the drainage pipe and leaned forward.

"BoBo!" I yelled across the water. I looked up and down the canal, hoping that somehow he had wiggled free. "BoBo!" I hollered, left and right. "BoBo!"

He was gone. The water was black and smooth as it rushed by. I stepped from the pipe to the bank and to the spot where BoBo had slept. I stooped down to touch the dirt. I thought it might be warm. Half buried in the sand was the stupid watch I had earlier put on his arm.

This could have been Pete, I thought. He would have listened to me if I told him to "guard it with your life." He would have been on this exact spot with his back to the alligator. He would have been watching me walk away. He would have been begging me to buy him a Slurpee and I would have been thinking: Buy it yourself. And then he would have been ambushed and bitten and dragged back into the water, into the alligator lair tunneled under the bank, and eaten.

Dad was right. I shouldn't turn my back on him. I should keep an eye out for him. I'm the older brother and it's up to me to help him. I shouldn't break his arm and let him knock his teeth out or punch him like I do. Suddenly, I thought he might be at the Pagodas' getting a naked woman tattooed onto his arm.

I grabbed my rod and reeled in the line. Pete, I'm sorry, but wherever you are, stay put, I said to myself. I'm coming. I ran full speed with my tackle box in one hand and the rod in the other. I kept my eyes on the ground, picking the spot for each foot, making certain that I got the most out of each step.

I reached our back yard. "Pete?" I yelled as I dropped my tackle box and reel. I stuck my head through the open kitchen door. Mom was mixing a pitcher of frozen juice. "Have you seen Pete?" I asked. I was panting.

"I thought he was with you," she said.

I took off, running around the Pagoda side of our house. I jumped the low hedge and made for their far yard.

There was Pete. He was kneeling on the top of their slide, trying to get a skateboard lined up under him. Down below, Frankie held the lighter-fluid-drenched Hula Hoop, and Suzie stood to one side with her thumb on the top of a cigarette lighter. They were ready to go up in flames.

"Pete!" I yelled. "Stop!"

I ran up to Frankie and yanked the Hula Hoop out of his hand and flung it as far as I could. Frankie gave me a shove from behind. I turned and got ready to jump him.

"He wanted to do it!" Frankie shouted at me and stepped back.

"It was his idea," Suzie said, pointing to Pete.

"That doesn't mean you should let him do it," I yelled.

I looked up at Pete. "Get down here. I have something terrible to tell you." He let the skateboard go down the slide and he took the ladder.

"BoBo was eaten by an alligator."

He looked up at me. "Are you lying?" he asked.

"No," I said. "He was eaten by a ten-foot alligator that could just as easily have eaten you."

"He had fleas," Pete said. "I hate fleas."

"Don't you get it?" I said. "He was *eaten* by an alligator."

"I know what an alligator is," he said, then added, "BoBo smelled bad."

"He was your dog!" I yelled. "He worshipped you."

"He ate my shoes," Pete said.

"Don't you get what I'm saying?" I said.

"Get what?" he said.

"No wonder I have to take care of you," I said.

He stepped away from me. "Do you want to see my tattoo?" he asked.

"What!" I hollered. *"What?"*

"Just kidding," he said and began to laugh.

"Give me your other arm," I demanded. He stuck it out and I dragged him all the way home.

has gone nuts
in this house.
First we've never had
central air condition-
-ing. So mom and
Dad are always say-
ing that air con-
ditioning is bad
for your health.
But then the
first thing
say w
ready
hous
ha
Th

s
it
s

But no

**COCOA
BEACH**

"**E**VERYBODY PUT ON your best clothes," Dad said. He had just told us he was offered a high-paying job with a big construction company in Cocoa Beach, Florida. "We're going out to dinner and you can order off the expensive side of the menu."

"All right!" Pete yelled.

Betsy was suspicious.

"Don't give me that look," Dad said, turning toward her. "I talked with the boss today and it's in the bag."

"I didn't say a word," she said with indifference. "It's just that seeing is believing."

Mom gave him a kiss. She was three months pregnant and touched her belly with both hands when she leaned forward. "Don't mind her," Mom said. "It's a stage she's passing through." Then she gave Betsy a "straighten-up" glare.

"My ship came in," Dad said, shaking his head. "I've been waiting a long time, and now it's arrived."

"What about the dinner I cooked?" asked Betsy. She sounded hurt. She had made lima-bean soup. His favorite. "Cat-box soup" is what I called it. The smell of it nearly gagged me.

"We'll eat it tomorrow," he said while doing a smooth shadow dance around the living room. "Everybody knows soup is better the second day." Suddenly, he clapped his hands together. "Hey, let's go! I'm the dad and you are a family on the move." He smiled his big smile. The one I had seen when things worked out the way he said they would.

I ran up the hall and into my room. I put on a dark shirt, because I'm a slob when I eat Italian food. Once I wore a good white shirt and Mom made me wear a napkin tucked into my shirt collar with the ends gathered up over my shoulders. I looked like I was sitting in a baby chair with a bib on.

We went to the Venice Restaurant. It was decorated with murals of gondolas and churches and beautiful houses along a wide canal. Fort Lauderdale is known as the Venice of Florida because of our canals. But it did not look anything like the Venice I'd seen in books. Dad ordered a bottle of Chianti even before we sat down. Mom raised her eyebrows.

"This is a celebration," he announced.

"That's what I was afraid of," she said.

"I won't have to work two jobs anymore. In the evening I can come home, drink a cold beer, and read the paper with my feet up."

The wine arrived. The bottle was wrapped in straw like the ones we used at home for candle holders. "Glasses for everyone," Dad said to the waiter.

"None for me," Mom cut in. "I'll have a ginger ale."

Across the street, the old people lined up for dinner at
Morrison's Cafeteria. They all looked wealthier than we
were, so why were they eating there? All the food looked like
lawn clippings with hard-boiled eggs and sliced beets mixed
in.

Dad poured a little wine in each of our glasses, then raised
his to the ceiling. "Cheers," he said brightly. He looked
happy and hopeful. "To the future."

We all clinked glasses. The warm wine tasted like grape
juice and gasoline.

"Tell us about your new job?" Betsy asked.

"As soon as I know more, I'll tell you," Dad said and
poured himself another glass of wine.

"Then tell us more about Cocoa Beach," she said.

"It's a growing town. With Cape Kennedy aiming for
Mars, now there are a lot of jobs. The schools are good
because there are so many government brats in them.
There's a good hospital for Mom. The beaches are great,
and housing is cheap. What else can I say? The place is a
paradise. Oh, and I thought we could all drive up there some
day this week and look around."

"Great," said Mom, "I'll make some housing appoint-
ments."

"Houses are shootin' up like mushrooms," he said, "and
at good prices."

Betsy and I exchanged glances. If we went up during the
week, it meant getting out of school for one day, maybe two.
We were almost at the end of the school year. Betsy had been
saying her teachers were worn down and showing science
movies all day long. Mrs. Marshall still had us going in
circles. We were on our tenth copybook, and when we

weren't occupied with that, we were filling in the blanks on a mimeographed lesson plan she passed out. I could tell that she was sick of us; we were sick of her months ago.

The waitress came and we ordered. Once the food arrived, we didn't keep up the conversation. I was staring out into the future. What would it be like? I'll be going from elementary school to junior high. From having a few friends to having no friends again. From being a home renter to being an owner. Plus, there will be a new baby in the family. We already had lived in nine different houses. This was my fifth school out of six grades. Was this going to be a fresh start? Or was this only another beginning without an end, like all the others?

"Jack," Mom said to me, "pay attention to what you are doing."

I looked down at my dinner. I had twirled nearly the entire plate of spaghetti into a large knot around my fork.

"Maybe we should learn some table manners," Betsy said, "before we move into a new neighborhood, so that people don't think we were raised in a cave."

"Sorry."

Betsy shook her head. I knew she wanted us to make a good impression when we arrived. I agreed with her. I just had a hard time doing it.

On the way home everything looked different to me. The neighborhood had changed. Suddenly, it seemed so temporary, like the fake cowboy towns built for making movies. The flat fronts of the houses were all that seemed real. If I could look behind them, I was sure I'd find the walls propped up with two-by-fours.

When we pulled up into our driveway, I ran to the front

door and was relieved when the door opened and I was able to step inside and make it back to my bedroom. I looked at my bed and chest of drawers. I opened my closet. I reached under my mattress and touched my diary. Everything was exactly where I had left it. I knew it couldn't be any other way. But I felt different. Something in me had been flattened. The real me had already moved out of town, and the fake me was left behind.

Dad didn't want to go to Cocoa Beach over the weekend. He had tickets to the Jackie Gleason Golf Tournament in Fort Lauderdale. I didn't mind playing golf, but watching other people play was boring. Dad once took me to caddy for him. I dragged his clubs across eighteen miles of desert under a blistering sun. On every hole I asked if I could buy a Coke. He never took me again.

Some of the kids in the neighborhood talked about applying to be professional caddies at the tournament, but I didn't have enough experience. I walked over to the Pagodas' side yard with Pete. Frankie and Suzie were squirting lighter fluid down an ants' hole and setting it on fire. It looked like a tiny volcano erupting, and the lines of angry ants scattered like fleeing villagers. Frankie had a rubber model of Godzilla that he chased the ants with. He crushed one and screamed, "Oh no! Godzilla has flattened the emperor's son!"

"The Japanese Army is fighting back," cried Suzie. She squirted fluid on Godzilla and set him on fire. "Godzilla is on fire," she yelled, "and he's melting."

When Godzilla had turned into a glob of bubbling rubber, they lost interest in the game. "Hey," I said. "I have a great idea for our own golf tournament."

"We're not allowed to play golf," Suzie said.

"Why?" asked Pete.

"We were blasting tee shots down the hallway and one of the balls smashed against the fish tank and it exploded and all the water and fish went all over the dining room and my dad went ballistic and said we could never play again."

"But we'll play outside," I explained.

"We can't do that, either," said Frankie. "Before we blew out the fish tank, I smashed the windshield on the station wagon, and he went ape."

I couldn't believe I had discovered something that they were not allowed to do. And that it was *golf!*

"Do you guys want to go swimming in the pool?" Suzie asked. "We poured a bottle of dish soap in, so it's real bubbly."

I could see trouble. "I don't think so," I said to Pete and shook my head. "Are you sure you won't play?" I asked again.

"We can't even if we could," said Frankie. "We're driving up to West Virginia to pick Gary up from camp."

"From *prison!*" Suzie blurted out.

"Mom said to say *camp,*" Frankie said, and he punched her arm.

"I'll pour lighter fluid on you," she cried.

I grabbed the lighter fluid from her hand. "Stop it," I said and threw it to the other side of the yard. "Come on, Pete."

We walked back home. "Okay," I said. "We'll have a two-person tournament. We aren't gonna see any of these people again, anyway." We sat down on my bedroom floor with a big sheet of paper and a Magic Marker. "Here's the plan. We make our own golf course in the neighborhood. And it has to be tough. Like, we have to put a hole in all the most difficult yards."

"Okay."

I drew the neighborhood houses and wrote in the names of the people who lived in them. "You pick first."

"The Metrics'," he said. "Michelle gave me a chocolate, and after I ate it, she told me it was dog candy."

I put an X on their yard. I picked the Rooks' because of Gary's nasty mom. Pete picked the Diehls' because their mean Doberman pinscher was on a chain. I picked the Peabos' because Mr. Peabo drank too much and when he got sick Mrs. Peabo kicked him out of the house and he crawled around on the lawn and vomited all over. "Just think if your ball lands in a puddle of puke," I said and made a stinky face.

Pete picked the Irwins' because they had friends who belonged to a mean motorcycle gang. I picked the Gibbonses' because Mrs. Gibbons had yelled at me for throwing a rock at her mailbox. Pete picked the Pagodas' because Gary was coming home. I picked the cranky old couple, the "crazies," because they always yelled out their window at us if we cut through their yard. We didn't know their real name. "And we'll put the last hole at our house," I said, "because Dad will go berserk if he knows we are doing this."

Pete looked nervous.

"Don't worry," I whispered. "We're going to do all of this when Dad's asleep."

"What about alligators?"

"I'll handle them. What we need is equipment." I wrote up a list: coffee cans, tennis balls, golf clubs, orange spray paint, a flashlight, and a trophy. "We better use tennis balls instead of golf balls. We don't want to break anyone's windows."

I sent Pete to find coffee cans, while I went down to the Salvation Army Thrift Store. It was my favorite store because everything was so inexpensive. Plus, they had stuff that wasn't for sale in any other store. I wished Mom would let me decorate my room with the great old stuff they had. I wanted the matching lamps made out of carved Mexican dancers. They had old brass beds that were tarnished, or painted in the last century. Some of the furniture was futuristic-looking, as though it came out of the Jetsons cartoons. I really wanted the old dark furniture that had carved panels of men and women and animals and plants. They also had really old Spanish-style furniture that was half chewed by termites and so old-looking that Christopher Columbus might have brought it over. Plus, I knew some of it had secret panels. I rapped on all the spots I thought might open up and reveal a hidden treasure. But I only woke up a lot of termites.

I went over to the trophy case and picked out a huge golf trophy, and a smaller one for second place. It didn't bother me that a Mr. Justman had won the first one in 1947 and a Mrs. Lower had won hers in 1968. They were a dollar each.

When I returned home and showed them to Pete, he got excited. "I'm gonna win first prize," he said.

"Did you get the coffee cans?" I asked.

"I forgot," he said.

"What about the flashlight?"

He forgot that, too. "What have you been doing?" I asked.

"Watching the golf tournament on TV," he said. "I'm learning how to do it."

"Great idea," I said. "Maybe we'll see Dad in the crowd."

I sat down and stared intently at the gallery of people on the television. All those golf fans dressed in bright pink and lime green and pure white made my eyes hurt.

"Jack," Mom said when she came into the room. "Do you know what your father would say to you if he could see you watching him?"

I thought about it for a second. "No."

"He'd say, 'Didn't I tell you to mow the lawn today?' "

I groaned. "I'll get right to it."

On Sunday, we didn't have all our golf course built. We spray-painted the tennis balls and the insides of the coffee cans bright orange so we could see them at night. We scrounged through Dad's workbench until we found two batteries for my flashlight. Pete and I picked out a golf club from Dad's golf bag and practiced in the back yard. We put a can over on its side and tried to putt the balls into it. We took about ten shots each just to get across the back yard and into the can. "We'll practice this week," I said to Pete, "and next weekend we'll have the tournament."

"Great," he said. "When we move to Cocoa Beach, Dad said I could take golf lessons and join a golf club."

"Wow." I sighed. I was hoping for piano lessons. We hadn't been able to afford it, which upset me because I had a suspicion that I could be a great piano player if only I had the chance. I was the only kid I knew who asked his parents for piano lessons. All the kids who took them hated them and made fun of their teachers. I used to want to trade places with those kids and live their lives. But now I wouldn't have to feel like I wanted out of our family just because I wanted things we couldn't normally afford. Now I could have everything I wanted. I sat down on the grass and stared out into space. It felt good just to think that things were really getting better in the rich land of Cocoa Beach.

On Monday, I waited until after school to give my note to Mrs. Marshall. "Are you moving up to Cocoa Beach?" she asked after carefully examining my mother's handwriting.

"Yes," I replied. "My dad has a new job."

"I have a sister who teaches up there," she said.

"I'd be pleased to meet her," I muttered, thinking the opposite.

"I'll send her a letter telling her to expect you in the fall," she stated.

"Yes, ma'am," I replied. She had me trapped.

"And one more thing. Don't bring that diary into her classroom. You might spread a disease with all the dead things you keep in it."

I smiled. "Yes, ma'am."

When I got home, Mom was resting across the couch with her feet propped up on pillows.

"Are you okay?" I asked.

She whistled. "It's just hot out, and I'm feeling a little dreamy over Cocoa Beach. We're definitely going to get central air-conditioning in the new house." She looked around the room as though she was weighing in her mind what possessions should be thrown away and what things we would keep for the future. She looked at the terrazzo floor. "And we're getting wall-to-wall carpeting. And a dishwasher, and a washer and dryer that are in the house, and a nursery room for the baby."

Everyone was thinking about the future. It was the latest craze.

"Hey," she said, "you'd better stick around the house. Your dad's getting off work early and might need help packing the car."

"I'll be in the back yard," I said and stood up to run.

"After you put on your play clothes."

Having more money isn't going to change everything, I thought. Pete was in my bedroom looking over the golf map. "You ready to practice?" I asked.

"Ready whenever you are," he said. "I'll meet you out back."

We hadn't been practicing long when Dad drove up the driveway in a new Cadillac the color of tomato soup. "Now, don't get worked up," he explained to Mom when he saw her face. "It's a rental."

"Does it have a tape player?" Betsy asked. Music was becoming her entire life.

"Yep," he said cheerfully, "and you can use it."

That caught her by surprise. Usually, she had to argue with him if she wanted the radio on her station. "Don't trick me," she warned, "or I'll make you give me driving lessons."

"I hope you took out enough insurance on this," Mom said.

"You better believe it." He whistled. "These things cost a fortune."

"I have an idea," Mom announced. "Let's get a bucket of Kentucky Fried Chicken. It's too hot to cook."

I agreed. It was my week to wash the dishes, and every night Betsy had been burning the pots. I'd had to use a meat mallet to beat the blackened lima-bean crust off the soup pot.

"And we can eat in the car with the air conditioner on," she added.

"All aboard," called Dad. We jumped in and he backed out of the driveway, swung around in the street, and roared down the road. It felt so good to be sitting on the plush leather seats of the Cadillac, with the cold air blowing over

my face and hair. I wished everyone in the neighborhood
was standing by the side of the road when we passed. I'd
wave to them as if I were the Pope, and they'd wave back,
thinking: There goes the luckiest kid in the world.

After dinner, we stopped at a bookstore. Mom wanted to
buy some magazines to get ideas on how to decorate the new
house.

"Everyone gets to pick out a book," Dad instructed.

We had left the house so quickly that I hadn't put my
shoes on. "I don't think they'll let me in," I said to him.

"Nonsense. Those rules are for people who aren't buying.
We're paying customers, son. You can do as you please."

I'm living in a whole new world, I thought. Things are
changing so quickly. Last week, Dad would have said,
"Rules are rules. You'll have to wait in the car."

In the morning, we made the four-hour drive up route
A1A to Cocoa Beach. Normally, we left for every trip while
it was still dark, and we always packed food at home. But not
this time. When we arrived in Cocoa Beach, it looked like
every other Florida boom town. Everything was new, except
for a few ancient Spanish-style buildings that were crum-
bling and furry with black mildew. Most of the other cars
had license plates from different states. It was as if all the
families with the same dream had ended up in the same
town. "A lot of jobs opening up here," Dad said. "A lot of
money to be made."

We ate lunch at Denny's, and Mom called the real-estate
agent from a pay phone.

"Let's go," she said gleefully when she returned. "It's
house-hunting time."

We met the first agent on John Glenn Way. It was a new

housing development. The streets were named after the astronauts, and the avenues had names like Blastoff and Orbit. It was weird, but I liked it. I was hoping that the houses might be shaped like rockets and space stations, but they were pretty ordinary, except that they were new.

The agent walked us through each room of one house and explained all the features.

"We need five bedrooms," Mom informed her. "I don't want the kids to have to share rooms."

Pete shot me a happy look. I gave him the thumbs-up. If anyone would have to share a room, it would be me and Pete.

"Then I'll show you the deluxe model," the agent said with a smile.

We marched across the street. Deluxe did mean the best. There was a screened-in swimming pool and patio, with a small guest room separate from the main house. The kitchen was huge and had every appliance built in and up to date. There were five big bedrooms, two living rooms, and a formal dining room for entertaining. I overheard Mom say to Betsy that she'd need a maid to keep the house clean.

What kind of job did Dad get, I wondered. Maybe he will be building some secret rocket hangars for the space program. Maybe that's why he hasn't told us what he is really going to be doing.

We looked at a few more houses. One was on Shepard Place, and the other on Lunar Park. But after we saw the deluxe model, everything else looked too small.

It was getting late in the day. "Should we start back?" Mom asked.

"Let's drive by your new office," Betsy suggested.

"It's too far out of the way," Dad replied. "Why don't we stay at a motel? We can all take a swim and get some hamburgers and rest up for the drive home tomorrow."

Someone had switched our old dad with this new dad. A few months ago, he drove for thirty hours straight to Pennsylvania without a nap. Now he needed a full night's sleep to drive four hours. I wondered if I might get a bigger allowance.

The next morning, we were back home before noon. Dad dropped us off and drove the Cadillac to the rental office. He returned with his work truck full of empty liquor boxes. We stacked them up in the living room.

"I don't want you packing up all your clothes just yet," Mom instructed. "I do want you to pack everything you won't need in the next two weeks. That's when we move."

"We'll miss the last week of school," Betsy said sneakily.

"That's your bonus for helping me out," Mom replied. "Now get a wiggle-on."

I knew we wouldn't be packing unless we were really leaving. I was sorting through my closet when Betsy knocked on my door.

"What do you think is going on?" she whispered.

"My guess is that he has a great top-secret job with the government. Just like he said."

She narrowed her eyes. "I don't know," she said suspiciously. "Something smells rotten to me."

"But Mom seems to think it's okay."

"Mom is the one who got me worried. She doesn't know where the money is coming from, and Dad won't give her a straight answer."

"Well, ask him yourself," I suggested.

"I did. And he won't give me a straight answer, either."

I wanted everything to be as Dad said it was. It frightened me to think that he didn't have a great new job and that we weren't going to have a deluxe new house and a new car and new lives. "I think it's all okay," I said hopefully. "Dad wouldn't do something like this if he didn't think it was real."

"Oh, grow up," she groaned. "Why is he making such a mystery out of this?" She left with a sneer.

I don't know, I thought. Maybe he's been sworn to secrecy by the government.

On Saturday morning, Dad drove up to Cocoa Beach to check on his new job. Mom let Pete and me camp out in the back yard. Once we'd pitched his tent, we gathered up our equipment and made our final golf-tournament plans. With Dad out of the way, we didn't have to worry about him checking up on us. At midnight, we were ready.

The first hole was a par eight from our front yard, across and down the street, along the side of the Rooks' house. "I'll dig a hole and put the can in the back corner of their lawn."

"I'll put one in the Gibbonses' side yard," Pete said. "Par five."

We marked the planned hole locations on our maps. "Let's go," I whispered. We picked up our grocery bags of supplies and took off. The night was very quiet. A half-moon lit up the neighborhood, but we wore dark clothes and knew how to be sneaky from playing army games. I dashed across Gary's yard and with my spade dug a hole and inserted the can. I met Pete in the Gibbonses' yard. We continued on to the Peabos'. Pete crisscrossed over to the Irwins' and the

Metrics'. I did the Diehls' and the "crazies," and we met at the Pagodas', then buried the last can in front of our tent. "Did you have any trouble?" I asked.

"None," he said. "Everybody's asleep."

"Then let the games begin," I whispered.

I teed off. My ball hopped across the Veluccis' front lawn and stopped by the street. Pete had been practicing. He lofted his ball over mine and onto a neutral front lawn.

As I was about to play my second shot, we saw car lights heading our way. "Hit the dirt," I said.

We ducked down. The car turned and made for our street, then turned again at our corner. The passenger door swung open and a man fell out, rolled across the road, and stopped in front of where we were lying on the grass. The car kept going.

"It's Mr. Peabo," Pete whispered.

I reached out and shook his arm. He groaned. "Mr. Peabo," I said. "Mr. Peabo, speak to me."

He groaned some more. The car stopped and began to back up. Mrs. Peabo was driving. "Run," I cried. "She's lost it!" We jumped up and retreated behind a hedge.

"Lloyd," Mrs. Peabo said angrily as she got out of the car. "Get up! You're drunk."

He worked himself up onto his hands and knees. She opened his door and began to push him from behind. "Now move it," she growled, "before the whole world sees you." Then she kicked him in the butt. "You're nothing but a worthless drunk," she said and pushed him again. Slowly, like a sloth, he crawled forward and folded himself into the car. She slammed the door, then got into her side and drove up the street and into their driveway.

"Wow," Pete said. "He was drunk."

"Pickled." I whistled.

"Should we do something?" he asked.

"Let's just leave it alone," I said. "That's the beauty of moving. You don't have to get involved. Just pull up your tent stakes and move away like the nomads."

We continued the game. Pete scored a five on the first hole, and I scored a twelve. He beat me by a stroke on the Gibbonses' hole. We decided to skip the Peabos' house because Mr. Peabo was still stuck in his car and moaning. Pete beat me on the Irwins' and the Metrics'. I beat him on the Diehls'. We tied on the "crazies." From there, we had to fire a shot over the canal and into the Pagodas' back yard. It was about fifty feet across. I hit mine as hard as I could. It passed over the canal and landed out of sight. Pete topped his ball and it hit with a splash.

"Don't wake up the alligators," I cautioned.

We each carried a spare ball. His second shot reached the bank and bounced back into the water.

"Hand me your extra ball," he said.

"If this one goes in the water, you lose," I said, "and I get the big trophy." But he hit it squarely and it hopped across their side lawn. We crouched down and walked along the bank of the canal.

I knew there was no way I could beat Pete. While I'd been busy packing boxes, he'd been quietly practicing behind my back. I'd figured I could beat him at everything, but I was wrong. He was beginning to grow up.

We made our way around the end of the canal, then back down to the Pagodas'. We searched for the tennis balls but couldn't find them. "I'm going to turn on the flashlight," I whispered and pressed the button.

"Hey! What are you thieves doing sneaking around my yard?" hollered a voice from up in the trees.

I jumped back and froze. Pete turned and ran.

"Hey, come back here," the voice angrily demanded. It was Gary Pagoda. He was sitting in our tree fort, smoking a cigarette. "If you run, I'll make it worse on you," he threatened and threw a tennis ball at my head. He missed.

I didn't know what he'd do if he caught us. I didn't know what he had been taught in prison. I began to back away.

"You stay put," he ordered and jumped out of the tree. A cloud of gray smoke popped out of his mouth when he hit the ground. I took off. Pete was already out of sight.

"I said get back here!" he barked and threw the other ball at me. He missed again.

I didn't slow down as I jumped the hedge.

"I may not get my hands on you this second," he threatened, "but don't turn your back on me. I got a big knife and I'll get you when you're not lookin'."

I dove through the front entrance of the tent. Pete was panting. "We . . . can't . . . stay out here," I gasped. "He's gonna slit our throats in our sleep."

"Let's get inside," Pete said. "You first."

I threw myself out of the tent and crawled on all fours to the back door. Pete followed me, running with the big trophy held over his shoulder like a baseball bat. I yanked open the sliding glass door and let Pete in, then slammed it shut and locked it behind me. "Lock the front door," I ordered.

"Agghhhh!" he shouted and dropped the trophy. The little golfer broke off and skipped across the floor. "Gary stole a car and is coming up the driveway!" I spun around.

"What's that racket?" Mom called out from her bedroom.

The car door slammed. Somebody walked up to the door

and turned the knob. "Don't you dare come in," I shouted. "I'll call the police." I turned to Pete. "Dial 911," I ordered.

The door swung open. Pete yelped loudly. I dropped down into a karate crouch.

"What are you boys up to?" It was Dad, and he was angry.

"We thought you were Gary Pagoda," I babbled. I took a seat and tried to catch my breath. Mom wandered down the hall in her housecoat. Betsy followed.

"What are you talking about? And what the hell are you boys doing up this late at night?"

"I'm sorry, I'm sorry, I'm sorry," I chattered. "I'm so glad we're moving," I said between breaths. "I don't like living here anymore. Everyone is too weird."

"Why are you back?" asked Mom. "Is something wrong?"

Dad sat down on the couch and exhaled loudly. "Well," he said and leaned forward with his hands on his knees, "the bad news is that we're not moving to Cocoa Beach."

"What?" I shouted.

"Just slow down," Mom said.

"I knew it." Betsy crossed her arms. "This has all been too good to be true."

"Don't be so harsh," Mom said to Betsy. Then she turned to Dad and sat next to him. "Tell us what happened," she said evenly.

Dad took a deep breath. "They didn't get the military contract they expected," he explained. "So they won't be building the new airport and don't need to hire me. It just fell through, nothing more to it than that. I shouldn't have believed it until I saw the first paycheck."

"I thought you had already signed a contract," Mom said.

"Not yet," muttered Dad. "We only shook hands on it." He looked out at all of us. I felt the small beginning of a pain in my chest that wanted to grow.

Dad stood up and passed between us. "Let this be a lesson to you," he advised. "Never do business on a handshake. You'll get screwed every time."

"No kidding," Betsy mumbled.

I turned and went back to my room. I threw myself across the bed like something that had been tossed away. The future looked like more of the past. I imagined Johnny Foil flying his airplane and how good he must have felt, looping through the air, until suddenly he collided with the film plane and crashed to the ground in a ball of flames. Gary Pagoda can't kill me now, I thought, I'm already dead.

It took me a long time to calm down and begin to imagine how disappointed Dad must feel. Then Mom and Betsy and Pete. Feeling this terrible for losing something that we didn't even own yet was hard to understand. It wasn't like losing money out of my pocket. It was more invisible, like losing hope.

In the morning, we all walked around the house like zombies, with red, worn-out eyes. Mom and Dad looked through the "Houses for Rent" section of the newspaper. After they circled a few ads and made a few telephone calls, they climbed into the truck to inspect the houses. When they returned, Mom seemed relieved. "Well, we found a nice house," she announced.

"Where?" Betsy asked. The location determined our next school.

"On Eighth Street, in old Fort Lauderdale," she said. "I always loved it down there because the trees are so old."

"That means I go to Sunrise Junior High," I blurted out. It was a school filled with kids like Gary Pagoda.

"I'll be going to Fort Lauderdale High," Betsy said happily. "If I had to go to Plantation High, I'd run away and join a convent."

"Why?" Mom asked.

"It's a suburb full of morons," Betsy said.

"Actually, we looked at a house out there today," Mom said and plopped down in a chair. "We didn't like the people we'd be renting from. They had a beer keg next to the television, and they owned a pit bull."

"Those dogs are killers," I said, kneeling down and pulling her shoes off. Her feet were swollen.

Betsy ran into her room to use the telephone so she could tell her friends that she'd still be in town.

"Where will I go?" Pete asked.

"There is a school down the street," Mom said, fixing his hair with her fingers. "You can come home and eat lunch with me and the baby each day."

While Mom took her nap, Pete and I took down the tent. Frankie Pagoda came running over when he saw us.

"You guys won't believe this," he blurted out. "Gary stole our car last night and he's just been caught in Georgia."

"We saw him last night," I said. "We passed through your yard and he tried to kill us."

"Yeah, he showed me his knife."

Mr. Pagoda called for him. "Gotta go," Frankie said. "We're picking him up again."

I wished they would leave Gary in jail until we moved away.

After dinner, Mom was hot. "Let's take a drive along the beach," she suggested. "That always cools me down."

"Sure," said Dad. "Jack, Pete, you boys put the lawn chairs in the back of the pickup, so your Mom can sit back there and get a breeze."

I loved setting up house in the back of the truck. We loaded up the lawn furniture and filled a small cooler with ice and a jug of lemonade. We brought plastic cups and pillows. "Ready," we shouted.

"Let's go by the new house," Betsy said.

It wasn't far away. It was an old Spanish-style house with a red tile roof. Some people were still living in it, so we couldn't go inside. There were two tall palm trees in the front yard. They seemed to be a hundred feet high. I looked up at them. At that moment, the wind blew and a heavy brown coconut broke away and fell onto the sandy yard with a thud.

"We better have the coconuts cut out of the trees," Mom said. "They could hit one of the kids and really hurt them."

"Nay," Dad replied. "They're so hardheaded, the coconut'll just bounce off."

I could already see my first chore. Plus, the lawn was worse than where we now lived. There were so few tufts of grass that mowing the lawn will create a sandstorm. I'll have to wear a turban on my head. The hedges hadn't been clipped and had grown up over the windows. And I knew Mom would make me scrub the mildew out of the cracks in the ancient stucco walls.

We drove along the beach and cooled down with the sea breeze, then turned up Broward Boulevard. We were almost home when Dad turned into the drive-in theater and pulled over. "Look," he said excitedly and pointed up at the theater sign. *"The Sound of Music* is finally gone!"

"Yeah," I shouted. *"Planet of the Apes* is playing!"

"I wanna see it," Pete shouted.

Dad paid and we entered. We found a good spot in the middle and he parked the truck backward, with the lawn furniture facing the giant movie screen. Everyone took their seats and I poured out cups of lemonade. A Bugs Bunny cartoon was playing. Bugs glued Elmer Fudd's shoes to the floor, then pulled his nose until it stretched far enough down the street to tie it in a bow around a blacksmith's anvil. Then Bugs let it go. The anvil blasted up the street and hit Elmer square in the face and drove him through a barn. But after Elmer pulled his face out of the hole in his head, he was back on his feet, and once again he was chasing that rabbit down the street.